# Bliss

By

B.A. Talarico

&

Smurf

# DEDICATION

*I want to dedicate this book to my family and friends who have been here through it all. I want to make a special shout out to the people who made this possible:*

*Mackenzie Propst (main editor)*

*Kris Frigga (cover designer)*

*Marguerite Tomlin (assistant editor)*

*Claudette Melanson (print copy formatter & proofreader)*

*And last but not least, Smurf for the knowledge and insight into a world not known to me.*

# PROLOGUE

The sky is cloudless, as the morning rays beam down. A gentle, eighty-degree breeze blows, creating sensations that make skin feel as if the lips of an angel were gently kissing it. The clear, blue ocean and white sands are breathtaking.

"JJ, would you mind rubbing some suntan lotion on us?" the beautiful, tanned brunette says with a seductive grin.

He removes his sunglasses and looks at the blonde and brunette beauties. "Sure, Sissy."

Both ladies remove their bikini tops and prepare themselves for the touch of his strong hands. To most men, he is living a fantasy beyond his wildest dreams. He is young, wealthy, and very powerful.

Yet even with everything, he is not happy.

He owns a very large oceanfront villa tucked away in Los Cabos.

It's an amazing house with architectural design that would make some of the richest people on the planet jealous. The house is located on two acres of oceanfront land. It takes up 10,000 square feet, with five bedrooms and five and a half bathrooms. Three of those bedrooms are in the main house, and the other two are in the guesthouse. No detail was overlooked when he initially bought this house. The master bedroom even features a large wall of pocket doors that open to a One-hundred foot private ocean frontage, but that wasn't enough. The large outdoor living space has a large pool with a swim-up bar, outdoor kitchen, and a large movie theater. He also has a garage where he keeps his transportation, which includes a mix of exotic cars.

His real love is his home on the water, an Eighty-five-foot yacht with six staterooms, an elevator, and a large amount of outdoor space. On top of the best-of-the-best interior designs, it even has a helipad with helicopter, just in case of emergencies.

In the last two years, he has lived a life that has felt like a roller coaster ride. After all he's seen and done, never would he have imagined that a paradise such as his getaway spot would serve as his prison. Psychologically, it tortures him to know that what he wants most in the world can never again be obtained. He is in too deep. If he could go back to his old life and just be a regular college kid again, he'd give up all of these luxuries and all of this money...just to be free.

The irony is that he has created this prison. Life has forced him to shut the rest of the world out. It's safer that way and the only way to protect his loved ones. What he wouldn't give to see his mother and father again.

His phone rings, interrupting his thoughts. "It's time to move again," the familiar voice says over the phone.

He has come to trust Smurf and doesn't hesitate to answer. "I'll be ready," he says, then disconnects the call. He looks at the beautiful women as they kiss and touch each other. He put his aviator sunglasses back on and leans back in his chair. The thought that comes to his mind is probably the most repetitive thought he has endured for as long as he can remember. *"How did it come to this?"*

# FLASH BACK

*Buzz, buzz.*

A sexy voice spills from his phone speaker. "Wake up JJ, you have class!"

*Buzz, buzz.*

"Wake up JJ, you have class!"

JJ raises his hand and smacks his phone. "Ugh," he sighs as he gets out of bed. Just as he swings his legs over the edge, the door opens.

It's his roommate Mark, who is tall and tan with short brown hair and an average body build.

"Yo, JJ. You just getting up, Bro? It's 9:00 in the morning!"

"I know," he replies. "It's my lazy day."

Mark just looks at him and laughs. "With the way you go to class, that's every day!"

"Yeah, you laugh, but I'm still getting straight As, Mark."

"True, but get your ass up! Are we going to smoke a blunt later or what?"

"Yeah Bro, my connection gave me a sack of purple kush to try when I went to go pick up some more X-pills."

"Good, now get your ass in the shower," Mark responds as he laughs and leaves the room.

After showering, JJ tosses on a pair of sweats and a T-shirt, grabs his backpack, and heads to the bus. He gets dropped off at the library. Standing out by the front door talking to a group of girls is a short, sexy beauty with long brown hair and olive skin. Her teeth are perfect and make her hazel eyes pop. She is wearing a pair of skintight Coogi jeans and an Iowa State T-shirt that shows off her perfect pair of breasts.

"Damn, Stacy! Look at you, looking sexy as hell… What's the special occasion?" JJ asks.

Stacy laughs. "No special reason."

"Well, looking sexy like that might make it hard for me to concentrate. I need to be able to focus if I'm going to help you with chemistry."

Stacy smiles. "Come on, JJ. You're getting 95% in that class…and you're a member of Lamda Lamda Lamda. That frat is full of nothing but 'A students' that party every night. I don't think anything could distract you enough to not be able to teach me how to do this stuff."

He flashes a grin. "Yeah, you're probably right. Let's get going."

They make their way up to the third floor and find an empty table. He's there to help her with chemistry, but he can't help stealing glances at her when she's writing. "Hey, JJ?"

"Yeah, Stacy. You got a question?"

"Well I do, but it's not about chemistry."

JJ gives her an awkward look. "Okay, what is it?"

"Well, we've gone to school together for a few years now and had quite a few classes together, but I know nothing about you."

He puts his pencil down and turns to her. "Alright, so what do you want to know?"

"What do you like to do? What type of music do you like? I know you're smart, and you are originally from Chicago, but that's it."

JJ laughs. "Well, when I was younger, my parents made me buckle down on school, but as I got older, school got easier, and as my grades stayed up, I started partying a lot. When I turned 18, I was hitting some of Chicago's hottest nightclubs: Prop House, Biology Bar and Velocity, you name it. I'm really into electronic music. Whenever I'd party, I'd take ecstasy because I was too young to drink."

"What?" Stacy responds. "You take ecstasy?"

"Yes, I do. I don't really drink...just pop a pill and go party. Once you pop, the fun don't stop. That's my motto."

"That's crazy, JJ. You don't look like a guy that does drugs."

"Well, I don't plan to do it all my life. I'm just trying to have fun for a while."

"I guess you're right. You only live once, so enjoy it!

# SMURF

A hot summer night meets with loud music and screaming and kicks off one of the hottest concerts at the Mansion Night Club in South Beach, Miami.

Smurf, all dressed up in a white linen academic outfit with a brand new pair of all white Js, holds a blunt in one hand and a vodka cranberry in the other. As he sips and smokes in the V.I.P section, he looks over the club, watching as the crowd roars and T.I. performs.

He takes a sip of his drink and thinks back on how much his life has changed. He remembers back to the day when he was in the hood in South Chicago, standing on the corner hustling bags to the smokers, when his partner Yeo, a skinny, dark-skinned kid with corn rows and baggy Echo clothes, shows up. "What's up, Fam?"

"Sup, Yeo," he responds as they do their secret handshake.

"Smurf, man, I'm looking for some bud. You got any?"

"Nah, man...but Old Man Smoke around the corner got some killer bud."

"Can you take me there?"

"Yeah, I got you. I need to grab a couple of bags for myself anyways."

As they reach the run-down, brick building, Smurf approaches the number pad by the door and pushes the button to apartment number ten.

"Is that Old Man Smoke's apartment?" Yeo asks.

"Yeah Yeo, so now you know."

"Hello," a deep voice says over the intercom.

"Hey, Smoke. It's Smurf. You good up there?"

"Yeah, come in. See you in a minute."

They walk in and head to the apartment. Smurf pounds on the door. The door opens, and an older man, about fifty years old with tattoos covering his arms and a small salt-and-pepper afro, looks out. "What's up, Young Blood?"

"Shit, nothing Smoke. Just needing to re-up."

"How much you need, Young Blood?"

"Can I get three for a quarter? I don't know what he wants," he says as he motions towards Yeo.

"Nigga, I want it all!" Yeo yells, punching Old Man Smoke in the face. Smoke falls to the ground. Smurf can only watch as Yeo begins kicking the old man in the face with his Timberline boots. With each kick, blood begins to pour from Smoke's face. Once unconscious, Yeo grabs all of Smoke's weed.

"Run!"

They bolt, sprinting down the hallway. Once outside, they run to the backside of the building to catch their breaths. "What the fuck, Yeo? What the fuck you rob his ass for, Fam?" Smurf shouts between breaths.

"Dawg, I'm hit man. I need the money."

"But Smoke would have helped your ass! You didn't have to beat his ass and take his shit! But hey, that shit is on you now. You best believe his son gonna be looking for your ass."

"Fuck Smoke Jr.! That nigga ain't shit anyways." Yeo takes a couple bags from his stolen stash and tosses them to him. "Here's some weed for helping me out."

Gun shots ring out in the calm night air. "Shit!" the two yell as they both duck for cover. They hear a man yelling from what seems to be the apartment above around the corner of the building.

"Where you bitch ass nigga's at! Wanna steal my shit? I got something for your bitch asses!"

After that night, a week or so goes by with no problems. One day while Smurf is standing at a corner hustling, a group of guys all dressed in black run up and begin jumping him. As he lay on the ground, trying to reach for his pistol in the waist of his pants, he takes a kick to the face. He is bleeding and dazed. Through the mental fog, he hears one man speak. "That's for robbing my dad, Bitch." Another kick to the face opens up a cut just above his right eyebrow. The men scatter. Blood drips into his eye as he watches them run.

*I'm gonna kill that nigga Yeo when I catch his ass, and I'm gonna kill that nigga Smoke for sending his bitch ass kid my way, too.*

The following night he is cruising around the hood in his black-on-black Chevy Tahoe, trying to figure how he's going to get back at Smoke and his kid, when he sees Robbie. He remembers that Robbie used to sell for Smoke.

*This is my way in...he'll get me in the door, I know it.*

He slows down as he approaches Robbie and rolls down his window. "Yo Joe. What's up, Family?"

"Shit," Robbie replies.

"Shit? You wanna smoke a blunt?"

"Fuck yeah!" Robbie replies, as he hops into the front seat of the

SUV.

After driving for a few minutes he asks, "Robbie, you still selling weed?"

"Yeah, why what's up?"

"Well this is my last blunt Fam, and then I'm out. Can you get me some?"

"Yeah, but we gotta stop by Smoke's spot."

"Alright," Smurf replies.

*This shit is gonna work.*

After rolling up to the apartment, Robbie pushes the number ten and waits for an answer.

"Who is it?" the voice says over the intercom.

"It's Robbie, Smoke. Let me in."

The buzzer rings, and he opens the door. Smurf takes a few deep breaths.

*It's now or never. You're right here. Do this shit and dip.*

He follows Robbie toward the apartment. Robbie begins to bang on the door, unaware Smurf has his pistol out and hanging to his side behind him. As the door begins to open, Smurf shoves Robbie into the door and into the dirty, dimly lit, run-down apartment and closes the door behind him.

"What the fuck, Smurf?" Robbie says, and then goes quiet when he sees the gun.

"What you want, Nigga?" Smoke says. The old man sees the gun and his eyes narrow. "Young Blood, you don't have the balls to do shit with that piece."

"You think so, huh?" Smurf says, keeping the gun on Smoke.

"I know so, Young Blood. You're just a punk." As the word 'punk' comes out of his mouth, Smurf lays one round into Smoke's leg, shattering his kneecap.

"Fuck!" Smoke yells.

"Damn, Smurf! What the fuck?" Robbie yells.

"Shut the fuck up, Robbie! So what was that, Smoke? I didn't have the, what did you say?...balls to shoot you?"

"Fuck you, Smurf! You're a dead man! My son will have your head for this!"

"Really? Actually Smoke, where's that little nigga at anyways? Let's have him stop by so I can take care of his bitch ass with you."

"Fuck you, Smurf! I'll get the last laugh!" he yells as he tries to tend to his wound.

"Nah, Nigga, you won't," Smurf says as he lays another round into Smoke. This one pierces his heart. As the sound from the gun echoes in the living room, Smurf can almost see the bullet traveling in slow motion into Smoke's chest.

Robbie tries to run, but Smurf fires one shot into his back, throwing him to the ground. "No Smurf, please," Robbie pleads.

"No witnesses," Smurf says as he shoots Robbie in the head. Smurf watches as the back of Robbie's head splatters onto the wall behind him.

He begins to search the apartment one room at a time, making sure no one else is there. As he reaches the bedroom, he hears a creak from the front room. When he goes to look, he catches the back of a person scrambling out the front door.

As he rushes to the front, he sees a woman sprinting down the hallway. He figures this to be Smoke's wife. Either way, he can't afford to take any chances. He fires a wild shot that just barely catches her in the back of the leg, but forces her to tumble to the ground.

"Please don't kill me. I won't tell anyone," she pleads as she curls into the fetal position.

He responds with a cold, emotionless expression. "Dead people can't tell," he says. He fires one final shot into her face from point-blank range. He's so close in fact that the fire from the bullet singes her face and hair.

As her body slumps to the ground, he sprints toward the exit. He hears a door open as he runs past. He fires a few wild shots behind him, but he can't tell if he hit anyone. He reaches his SUV and speeds off down the street.

*Don't think about that. That nigga Yeo... I'm going to kill his ass next for getting me dragged up into this mess.*

# JJ

The view in a dimly lit lecture hall is the last thing JJ wants to see at 8:30 in the morning. The sight of 500 people laughing and talking while waiting for the teacher is annoying him. He can smell the scent of alcohol and cigarette smoke on the students sitting around him. That smell mixed with the heavy smell of cologne and perfume is almost unbearable. It actually starts to cause a migraine just behind his eyes. He slouches over in his chair with his MP3 player, playing a mix he made the night before to keep him awake while he waits for the class to begin.

"Good morning, Class. Where did we leave off?" the teacher asks as he enters. "But before we get started, let's have everyone click to sign in."

Students around him pull out their clickers and start entering their numbers. JJ watches as the numbers start to appear on the screen behind him. He keeps his eyes locked, waiting for his number to appear. "There it is," he says under his breath.

In the middle of the lecture, he feels his leg vibrate.

*Who could be texting me at 8:30 in the morning?*

He pulls out his phone and flips it open. *Oh...Dad.* He reads:

JJ call me when you get some free time I'm free till ten.

He closes his phone and looks up at the information the teacher is covering.

*Man this shit is bogus. I'm out of here.*

He excuses himself as he stands up and exits through the back of the room. Once outside, he reaches back into his pocket and pulls out his phone to call his dad.

"Hey, JJ," the deep, masculine voice says after a few rings.

"Yeah, dad...you needed me to call?"

"Yes, I wanted to see what you're doing for Spring Break."

"I'm not sure. Why do you ask?"

"Well, your mom and I haven't seen you for a while, and we would love if you came home and spent some time here."

"Yeah, that's fine. I don't have any plans. I'll come home for Spring Break."

"Okay, great. I'll tell your mom that you'll be coming home."

"Okay. I'm going to get going. I'll talk to you later, okay? Love you.

Tell Mom I love her, too."

"Okay, I'll tell her."

After hanging up, he heads toward the McDonald's in the basement of the union. After getting his meal, he heads to a corner table overlooking the room. He watches as a few people sit, eating and talking, while others stand in line at the different fast food chains across the room.

While consuming his meal he hears, "Yo, JJ." He looks up to see Mark standing in the middle of the front door. He nods as Mark starts to walk toward his table.

"Hey J, you didn't go to class today?"

"Nah, I couldn't handle it today. I hate history. What the hell do I need to know about history for as a chemistry major? I still can't figure these people out. Just wanting money, I guess."

"Yeah, but lucky for you J, school comes easy for you."

"Yeah, but it sucks. I get bored, and I want more out of life than this. I dream of the luxury lifestyle, doing what I want when I want."

"We all do. One day you'll be there. You just have to do this first."

"I know, but I hate to wait, Bro. So, what are we going to do tonight? I was thinking about heading to Club E. What do you think?"

"Yeah, it's Thirsty Thursday, so the club will be packed tonight. I'm waiting for my connection to get back into town so we can have some party favors for later."

"Will he be back in time for the club?"

"Yeah, he'll be back here in the afternoon some time. Alright...well, I got to go to class, J. I'll see you later."

"Okay, Mark. Have fun. I think I'm going to go workout for a bit."

As Mark heads out of the food court, JJ throws out his trash and makes his way to his car to drive to the gym. He just starts his workout when he receives a call on his cell.

"Hello?"

"Hey, JJ. You busy?" the voice asks.

"Well, I'm working out right now. You back in town?"

"Yeah, I'm back at home. Stop by when you're done."

"Okay, I'll see you soon," JJ says and hangs up.

He finishes his workout, drinks his protein drink, and heads to the car. He makes his way to a small, two-story, brick apartment building with white pillars and red wood doors on the outside of each apartment. He pulls out his cell and redials.

"Hey, Leon. I'm here."

"Okay, the door is open. Just come in."

JJ walks up to the door with the number forty-five on it, walks in the front door, then shuts and locks it behind him as he makes his way to the living room.

"Hey, JJ. You locked the door when you came in, right?"

"Yeah I did," he responds. As he gets closer to the couch where Leon is sitting, he sees his large forty-two inch flat-panel TV mounted to the wall with Call of Duty Four action playing on the screen. He sits down on the dark-brown leather couch, looks at the glass table, and sees Leon, a young guy in his mid-twenties with short, dirty-blonde hair and olive-colored skin, dressed up in polo T-shirt and plaid shorts.

"So did you get those for me, Leon?" he asks. He watches as Leon pauses the game and pulls out a large Ziplock bag and sets it on the table. "Holy shit!" JJ responds as his eyes widen. It looks like a bag of Skittles with all different shapes, colors, and sizes of ecstasy pills. "How many pills are in there?"

"Somewhere close to like, 20,000 or so."

"So which ones are the best ones?"

"The best ones I tested with my EZ-test chemical tester are these ones," Leon says as he pulls out a white ecstasy pill and lays it on the table.

JJ picks up the pill and examines it. "Hey, this has the mud flap girl like you see on all the trucks.

It also has a stamp on the back of a dot and a 'G' next to it. Why does it have two stamps, Leon?"

"I'm not sure. I was told they come from New York and the 'G' represents some club called The Guardian or something...but they call them Lady Kappas on the street."

"So these are the best ones you have?"

"Yeah, you want them?"

"Yeah!"

"How many?"

"Well, I usually get like ten, but I was wondering if I could get a few more to try to make some money selling them."

"How many do you want?"

"Well, can I get like, one hundred?"

"Yeah, that's fine. Go ahead and count out one hundred ten pills."

"Why one hundred ten?"

"Well, you sell the one hundred and eat the ten for free. I do that with anyone I mess with because you're making me money, and you're making yourself money, so a few free ones won't hurt anyone."

"How much do I owe you for the one hundred?"

"Just give me $500 for those. It's funny, JJ... I still remember when I started selling pills. I was just like you, just wanting to party, have fun and enjoy life. Then the business end kicked in. I realized...for all the money I was spending, I could be selling and having fun. I soon realized there is a lot of money in this business, and I wanted a piece of it. So, I gave up the partying and started the hustling, and now look... I'm enjoying my life and making money doing it. Don't get me wrong, JJ... I don't want to do this my whole life. I'm just trying to save up enough to start my own business, and then I'm getting out."

"I know what you mean, Leon. I want a nice lifestyle myself. I hate having to go to school and be bored just so I can get my degree to make big money. I just want to live that life now."

"Baby steps, Little Cousin. You can't run before you walk, and I want to warn you now, this life has its own rules...rules you've never experienced before. If you're not strong enough, it can consume you and your livelihood."

JJ's phone rings. It's Mark. "Hey, Mark. What's up?"

"Hey, JJ. We still meeting tonight? Did you meet you-know-who?"

"Yeah, I'm here. Everything is good for later."

"Okay, I'll let you go then. Just checking."

"Alright, Mark. See you in a while." He closes his phone.

"You got some time?" Leon asks.

"Yeah, I do."

"Well, pick up that pipe, hit that Purple Kush, and let's play a few games of C.O.D."

JJ picks up the pipe and takes two big hits, filling his lungs.

*This is going to be a great day.*

-----

It's 9:00 that night and he's getting ready when Mark walks in. "Hey JJ, you almost ready?"

"Yeah Mark, are you?"

"Yeah. Hey, we going to smoke that Kush before we go?"

"Yeah. We're going to walk to the club anyways, so we'll smoke then."

"You got them pills for tonight?"

"Yep," he says and tosses the bag to Mark.

"Damn, you got a lot! How many is there?"

"one-hundred are in that bag. I'm going to try to sell them at the club tonight. You wanna help? I'm trying to sell them for $20 each. I'll give you $5 each for selling them, so you could make $500 tonight."

"Are you serious?"

"Yeah," he replies.

"Alright! Shit, I could use the extra money, too."

"Hey, Mark."

"Yeah, JJ?"

He pulls out another bag of pills. "These pills are for us tonight! I got ten pills, so that means we need to find some girls to fuck tonight."

Mark laughs. "For sure! This is going to be the best night of the year for us."

"We will just have to see. If all of these pills sell, it's definitely going to be a great day."

It's almost 10:00, and Mark sits with a blunt between his lips. in a chair in the living room, waiting. "Hey, JJ! You ready?"

"Yep," he replies from his room. "Light it up." He enters the room and sits on the couch. Mark takes a hit and passes it to him. He takes a bit hit and exhales through his nose. "Hey Mark, when you want to pop?"

"Shit, let's pop now," he says and laughs. "By the time we get to the club, we'll be rolling."

"Alright," JJ says as he pulls the small baggy from his coat pocket and passes a pill to Mark. He puts one on the table for himself and takes another puff from the blunt.

As he smokes, Mark goes to the kitchen and comes back with a glass of water and sits down. "Well, JJ," Mark says as he raises the glass. "This is to a great night of partying, money making, and hopefully great sex!" He laughs and tosses the pill in his mouth. He takes a big gulp and passes the glass to JJ.

JJ passes the blunt and accepts the glass. "To a night that we will remember forever." He tosses the white Naked Lady in his mouth and washes it down with the remaining water in the glass. "You ready to go?"

"Yeah, let's bounce," Mark replies.

As they leave the apartment, he checks his pockets to make sure he has all the pills. The apartment complex where they live isn't far from the club--about ten minutes in walking distance. By the time they arrive, the line is wrapped around the corner. The club is two floors, and he can hear the music playing outside.

"Hey Mark, is Jimmy working the door?" he asks.

"Lemme look...yeah, he is. Let's go."

As they head to the front of the line, Mark yells, "Jimmy Boy!"

Jimmy looks up and waves Mark and JJ toward the front entrance. "What up Mark," Jimmy asks.

"Shit, nothing Bro. Thanks for letting us in."

"Yeah, no problem. Anything for my Lamda Lamda Lamda boys."

Mark leans in close to Jimmy. "I got a bunch of X-pills, too...so send them my way if peeps ask.

I will be in the V.I.P by the DJ."

"Okay, will do, and have fun." Jimmy turns to JJ. "Hey, JJ!"

"What up, Jimmy?" he replies as he walks by with Mark.

As Mark and JJ walk up the red stairway to the first floor, they can see the lights flashing. Mark turns to JJ, "Man, I'm peaking."

JJ laughs. "Well, have fun in space!"

They enter the first room and it's packed wall to wall with people.

The dance floor is full of people dancing and grinding. Around the outside of the dance floor are the V.I.P tables, and even these are packed with people. Hanging from chains are flat-screen TVs showing videos as the music plays. He looks into the lights hanging from the ceiling and starts to feel the drug kicking in.

He walks up to the DJ booth next to the V.I.P tables. "Yo, what up DJ D-Tec?"

"Hey JJ, what's up?"

"Nothing. Hey, can you play that *Call on Me* song by Eric Prydz?"

D-Tec laughs. "Yeah, I can. Why? You rolling?"

"Ha, yeah...I'm starting to peak."

The DJ leans in closer. "You got any more?"

"Yeah, let me get one!" He reaches his hand in his pocket, pulls out a pill and passes it to D-Tec.

"How much I owe you?"

"Nothing...just if anyone wants some, send them to Mark. He's selling them."

"Alright, Bro, will do."

JJ turns and realizes he's lost Mark in the club. He makes his way to the bar on the first floor.

The pill is really starting to kick in now. The lights are starting to mess with his eyes. His entire body is so sensitive to the touch and the hair on his arms and neck are standing up. He feels like a million bucks, without a care in the world.

As he starts peaking, D-Tec comes over the music. "This is for my homeboys, JJ and Mark!"

All the lights go off as the track changes. The bass from the club music starts setting off strobe lights. Slow at first. As the music fades in, the strobes start going off faster and faster while the bass vibrates the whole club.

He is lost in the lights as the bass pulsates across his skin. He's peaking--sweating and loving it. The sensations are intense. It feels as if he's having an orgasm each time the bass hits and the strobe lights flash. He closes his eyes and gets lost in the music. He can feel it throughout his body, like an electric snake coiling its way around his body. "He starts dancing and moves out to the dance floor. Each time he bumps into a person, it sends ripples through his body.

*Jesus, these are the strongest pills I've ever taken...and where the hell is Mark? He is supposed to be helping me sell these things.*

The DJ comes over the sound system again. "Will my crazy ass homeboy JJ, come to the DJ booth! Mark is lost without you up here, so get your ass up here!"

JJ is still lost in the music, but manages to make his way to the DJ booth. Mark is standing by a table when he walks up.

"JJ, where the hell you been, Man? I was waiting by the bar... I even went to the second floor to scope out the dance floor, but I couldn't find you!"

"Man...Mark, I was lost in the lights and music. These are great!"

"Yeah, I know! That's why I've been trying to find you! I need ten pills."

He pulls out the bag and hands it to him. "Just take the bag and bring the cash back."

"Alright, man. Hey, hang out here in the V.I.P. I'm going to run around."

He takes a seat in the booth and pours himself some orange juice. While he sits on the couch, he hears his name being called, but his eyes are blurry from the pills.

A sexy, petite woman starts walking toward him in a bright-red, skin-tight dress. As she gets closer, he realizes it's Stacy.

"Hey, JJ! How are you?"

"I'm good, Stacy. You look sexy as hell in that dress!"

Stacy giggles. "Thanks. Oh hey, this is my friend, Amy."

A half-Spanish-looking girl with black hair smiles at him. She's shorter than Stacy and dressed in a white T-shirt and white mini skirt. "Hi, I'm Amy," the girl says, extending her hand.

He takes her hand and more ripples shoot through him. "I'm JJ. So you girls having a good time?"

"Well, we just got here. We haven't got a drink yet," Amy says.

"Oh, well, what you want? I'll go get it."

"Can I get a Bacardi Razz?" Stacy asks.

He nods, then looks to Amy again. "And for you, Amy?"

"Can you get me a Vodka Lemonade?"

"Yep. I'll be right back."

As he walks off towards the bar, Stacy leans in to Amy. She has to almost shout to make her words heard. "See, I told you what I read in Cosmo was true!"

"What's that?" Amy shouts.

"That if you wear red, men like to spend money on you!"

Amy laughs. "I guess you're right. So what do you think of JJ? He's cute!"

"Yeah he is, Amy, but he does ecstasy."

This seems to peak Amy's interest. "Really? Does he have any?"

"I don't know, why?"

"We should do it! I did it back in high school, and it was like having sex without actually fucking...and if you do have sex, it is so crazy intense!"

"Really?"

"Yeah! Ask him when he comes back!"

Stacy Is hesitant. "I don't know, Amy."

"Come on, Stacy! It's college! Time to try things, play a little."

He returns with the drinks. "Here's your Vodka Lemonade, Amy, and here's your Bacardi Razz, Stacy.

"Thanks, JJ," the girls reply.

"No problem."

Stacy takes a sip of her drink, then looks at JJ. "Hey JJ, can I ask you something?"

"Yeah, what's up?"

Stacy leans in to JJ's ear. "Do you have any ecstasy with you?"

He leans back. "Are you serious? I know you don't like to drink much...why do you want to roll? I just didn't think you did that type of stuff."

"Well I don't, but Amy wants to pop one with me."

"Well, the ones I got are strong, so you'll want to split it."

He pulls out a pill and breaks it in half with his teeth. He places one in Amy's hand and the other in Stacy's. Amy tosses it in her mouth and drinks it down.

Stacy is still hesitant. "I don't know, Amy."

"Don't worry, Stacy! You'll be fine with me and JJ!"

"Okay." Stacy tosses it in her mouth and drinks it down with her drink.

Thirty minutes pass, and JJ leans down to Stacy. "Do you feel it yet?"

"Well, I feel a floating sensation...and the lights are getting intense. Is this it?"

"You're starting to feel it, just wait."

He leans back on the couch, and Mark walks up. "Hey, JJ."

"Yeah, what's up?"

"Hey, how much do I owe you on those?"

"Why, did you lose them or something?"

"No, no, no, I got the cash for you!"

"You're shitting me!"

"No, I told you I'd get rid of them!"

"Well, I need $1,500."

Mark sits down and pulls out a wad of cash from his pocket. He starts counting under the table.

"Hey Mark, you remember Stacy?"

Mark looks up from counting. "Oh yeah. Hey, Stacy."

"And this is her friend, Amy."

Mark pauses, then takes her hand. "Hi, Amy. Nice to meet you."

Amy smiles and nods. JJ leans down again. "Hey, you girls go dance. We'll be out there in a couple of minutes. Mark and I need to talk about something real fast." Amy grabs Stacy by the hand and leads her away. He turns back to Mark. "So, you got that cash?"

"Yeah." Mark pulls out a small stack from a wad and puts it on the table. He counts it out for JJ.

"Here's $200, $500, $800, $1,000, $1,300, $1,500. See, all there."

JJ grabs it quickly and puts it in his pocket, scanning the crowd to make sure no one saw the transaction.

Mark drops his head and laughs. "No one cares, dude! They're all drunk and partying!"

He takes a drink and sits back. "Hey Mark, what you think of Amy?"

"She's pretty hot. Why?"

"Well, I just gave them a pill. I want to dance with Stacy, and Amy needs a friend."

"Shit, I'm game! Let's go!" He and Mark make their way to the dance floor to find Stacy and Amy bumping and grinding on each other. Mark slides behind Amy and starts grinding with her while JJ slides up to Stacy and starts dancing.

"How do you feel?" he says into her left ear.

"I feel great! This is awesome... I didn't know this is how ecstasy makes you feel!"

He starts rubbing her arms and runs his fingers through her hair. Stacy closes her eyes and lets off a soft moan. She turns around and faces him and starts dancing up against him. He leans down and blows softly in her ear. The sensations send chills down her body, making her horny as hell. He lightly kisses her neck, and she grabs the back of his hand. The sensations are almost too much for her to handle.

"Hey JJ, let's sit down."

"Alright." He leads her back to the V.I.P. "How do you feel? Are you hot? We got bottles of water." He opens up a bottle and hands it to her. "Drink some."

Stacy takes a couple of big swigs. "Man JJ, now I know why you like this so much. It's so much fun!"

"See, I told you it's not as bad as you thought it was. What are you and Amy going to do after the club?"

"I don't know. Probably just go home. What are you and Mark going to do?"

"We'll probably head back to our place. You and Amy wanna come hang out?"

"I don't know. I'll have to ask Amy."

"Well, it looks like Amy will want to," JJ says as he points to the dance floor. Amy and Mark are standing along the outside of the dance floor, kissing passionately.

JJ waves to get Mark's attention. "Hey, Mark!" As Mark looks up, he waves him over. Mark and Amy walk over to the booth.

"What's up, JJ?"

"Hey, you guys want to go to the house after the club?"

"Sure, does Stacy?" Amy replies.

"Yeah, I wanna go," Stacy says.

The DJ comes over the speakers. "All you sexy people out here, it's last call for alcohol, so get your asses to the bar. It's your last chance!"

"Alright, you girls ready to go?" Mark asks.

"Yeah," Amy replies.

"Yeah, let's go," Stacy says.

As they leave the bar, Amy asks, "So, where do you guys live?"

"The Legend Apartments," Marks replies.

"Oh yeah? I heard those are pretty nice."

"Yeah, they are," he says.

They get to the apartment about 1:45AM. The apartment opens up directly into the living room. It's a typical college apartment, with a small couch, a few chairs, a small table that sits in the center of the living room, a thirty-two inch TV, and a small sound system. The kitchen starts at the edge of the living room with a counter, where high bar stools sit.

"Hey, you girls go have a seat on the couch, and I'll make you guys something to drink," JJ says. He heads to the fridge to make some drinks while Mark heads over to the stereo and puts on Pri yon Joni's iPod mix.

He returns to the living room with a couple glasses of orange juice. Here you go 'he says', and puts them on the small table. "So how do you girls feel?" he asks as he sits down in a chair next to Mark.

"Well, it's starting to fade off," Amy says.

"Oh yeah? Do you guys want to split another one?" he asks as he reaches in his pocket and pulls out the baggy of pills. He hands it to Amy.

Amy accepts and looks to Stacy. "Hey Stacy, let's both take one each."

"I don't know, Amy...you got me to take half already."

"Yeah, but I never do this! Come on, just one more! Trust me, I won't ask you to take anymore!"

"Okay, okay, okay," Stacy replies. "Just one more and I'm done."

She gives Stacy a big hug and squeals. "Yesss! Thank you, Stacy! I love you!" Amy pulls out two pills and hands one to Stacy with a glass of OJ. She keeps the other one and grabs the other glass of OJ. Amy tosses the pill in her mouth and drinks it down.

Stacy looks at hers with more hesitation. "Come on, Stacy. I promise, no more after this one," Amy says. Stacy takes a deep breath and puts the pill in her mouth and drinks it down.

"Oh hey, I'll be right back," JJ says as he leaves the room and goes to his bedroom. He returns a few minutes later with a small bag of Kush and a pipe and sits down. "I know you girls don't smoke, but Mark and I are going to smoke, if that's cool?"

"Yeah, go ahead," Stacy says.

"It's your house anyways," Amy adds.

He pulls out some weed and loads the pipe and passes it to Mark. "Here you go." Mark lights it up and takes a big hit and passes it back to him.

"Man, I like this beat," Amy says. DJ Tiesto's *Love Comes Again* bumps in the background. "Come on, Stacy. Dance with me." The girls start dancing and Amy looks at Mark and grabs his arm to pull him up to dance. JJ follows Mark and starts dancing with Stacy.

"How do you feel?" he asks Stacy again.

"I feel great, it's really hitting me now."

As they dance he slides his hands up and down her body. The sensations are making her horny again. She pulls his head to hers and kisses him. Stacy turns around and starts grinding her ass against his crotch. He runs his fingers through her hair and down to her waist.

As they dance, JJ looks over and sees Mark and Amy making out. He is lost in the music and feeling the sensations being sent though him by Stacy. He turns to look at Mark again, but Mark is already leading Amy to his room.

"Hey, Stacy?"

"Yeah?"

As she starts to turn around, he leans in and kisses her glossy lips. As he moves to her neck, he grabs onto her hand. "Come on." He leads her into his room. He pushes open the door and turns on the light.

"So this is your room...you got a radio? Can you turn it on, please?"

"Yeah." He walks over to his laptop and turns it on. His room is kind of small. A queen-size bed takes up most of the room, and he has a small computer desk where his computer sits, surrounded by family photos. He has chemistry-related papers posted to his wall and a poster of Alexander Shulgin above his headboard.

"You really like chemistry, don't you?"

"Yeah, I have a thing for making chemicals. I want to be like Alexander Shulgin."

"Who is that?" Stacy asks.

"He's the guy who created ecstasy...greatest chemist on the planet. Maybe one day I'll create something that will change the world forever, but the only thing I'm interested in now is you." He sits down on the bed and starts kissing her neck.

"I want to do this, but you're not going to think of me differently, are you JJ?"

He smiles and shakes his head. "No, just relax and let me take care of you."

"Okay," Stacy replies.

He makes his way on top of her and keeps softly kissing her body to her lower left leg and wraps it around his waist. He moves his hand back up her body, softly brushing her breast. As he does this, she lets out a soft moan and arches her back. He runs his fingers down her arm to her hand and pulls it above her head. He kisses softly up to her ear lobe and blows softly into her ear. He lightly bites her ear lobe and tugs on it.

"How does that feel?" he whispers.

"Ugh, I love it!" she moans. She grabs onto his belt with her free hand and pulls him down on top of her. She slides her hand up under his shirt, skimming her hand along his muscular back. She frees the hand above her head and grabs onto the bottom of his shirt, pulling it up over his head. She sees his strong, muscular chest and rock hard abs. She rubs her hands up and down his upper body and hooks onto his strong shoulders and pulls him down on top of her again.

He starts slowly grinding against her. She grabs onto his hair and pulls his head down to hers. She starts biting his ear lobe. He takes her hands and pushes them above her head and slowly kisses her from her neck down to the upper part of her breast.

As he does this, he slides his hand down her arms to the top of her dress. He slowly pulls the straps of her dress down toward her belly button, kissing, licking and sucking on her neck and chest. He slowly pulls the dress more and finally reveals her Quarter-sized nipples that are hard and fully erect.

He slowly massages her left breast as he lightly licks around her right nipple, stopping to suck on it before nibbling. Each time he does this, she moans a little louder and arches her back.

"How does this feel?" he asks.

"Oh God, don't stop, keep going," she moans.

He kisses and licks his way over to the left nipple and flicks it with his tongue. He starts sucking and nibbling, just as he did to the right. He slowly pulls her red dress top down past her belly button. She closes her eyes and starts biting on her knuckle of her right index finger.

He keeps sliding his face down her body, but keeps his hands focused on her breasts. She pushes his head down to her pussy, but he keeps going down her legs to her feet.

He starts sliding his hands up each leg toward her pussy. Each movement sends shivers up her body, making her moan and squirm as his hands reach under her dress.

He grabs her black, g-string panties and slowly tugs them down her legs. He tosses them on to the floor as he slides his hands up Stacy's legs back under her dress. This time, his head follows his hands.

*This is the sexiest pussy I've ever seen, freshly waxed, bald, with not a hair in sight.*

As he pulls apart her lips and starts flicking her clit with his tongue, he starts slowly spelling words out.

Stacy is moaning louder now, "Faster, JJ!" He speeds up, licking faster in circles.

"Oh God!" she screams. He keeps licking faster and harder. He grips her legs as her body shakes from her first approaching orgasm. "Oh fuck, JJ. I'm going to come!" He grips harder and licks faster. She grabs onto his hair and pushes his head into her pussy. She lets off a loud moan, "I'm coming! I'm coming!"

As her body pulsates he keeps licking, feeling her pussy tighten and loosen. Her first orgasm. He licks his way up to her breasts and starts licking around her nipple in circles. She grabs his head and pulls his face to hers. She begins kissing him, this time using her tongue, tasting the orgasm she just left in his mouth. She grips him tightly. "I've never had an orgasm like that," she says, trying to catch her breath.

"Just think, we just started," he replies.

She rolls him over onto his back, straddles him and pushes his hands onto both of her breasts, she slowly starts grinding her body against his. As she lies down on top of him and lightly kisses his neck, she makes her way down his firm pecks and lightly bites his nipples, One and then the other. She starts following the trail of rock hard abs down past his belly button to the button on his pants. With her face buried in his groin, she unbuttons his pants and slowly pulls the zipper down with her teeth.

As she reaches the end of the line, she tugs his pants down by the pockets, leaving his boxers on. She slides her soft hands over his boxers and begins rubbing her hands all over his cock. "How does that feel?"

"That feels good."

"How good?"

"Really good."

He pushes back her hair so he can see her face down by his groin. She lightly bites his cock through the fabric and slides her left hand up his leg to his balls.

She starts slowly massaging his balls as she kisses his cock through his boxers. He lets off a deep moan. She grabs the top of his boxers and pulls them down to his ankles. He kicks them to the ground.

She lies between his legs and spreads them a little farther apart so she can kiss her way up his legs.

Making her way to his semi-hard cock, she takes a soft grip on it. She loves that he shivers at her touch.

She pushes the shaft of his cock toward his stomach and focuses on his balls, gently licking and sucking. This makes him fully erect, and he lets off another moan. She licks from his sack, slowly up the shaft, to the v-indention on the head. She licks around the head of his cock and slowly puts it deep into her throat, until her nose touches his stomach.

She starts moving faster and faster, up and down on his cock. He really starts moaning now and has his hands in her hair, allowing him to watch. She pulls his cock out of her mouth and smacks the head against her lips a few times and sticks it back into her mouth. She is sucking like a pro. He lets off a long moan and pushes her off him.

This surprises her. "What's wrong?"

"Sorry, I almost came. I needed you to stop before I did."

She smiles. "Oh, so I'm good then?"

"Yeah, the best head I've ever had," he says, still rock hard. "Okay, I'm good now."

She slides up to his cock. "Close your eyes, and no peeking."

She puts his cock straight up in the air and straddles above it. She starts to slowly lower down onto the head, taking him in. He opens his eyes and grabs onto her hips to help her down. As he enters her, she closes her eyes and leans her head down.

"Give me a second," she moans. "Just leave it in. Man, your cock's thick, JJ. I almost can't handle it, but it feels so good inside me."

She slowly starts riding up and down on him, moaning on each pump she gets. He pulls her down as she keeps riding him. He starts sucking her nipples and kissing her neck.

He moans in her left ear, causing her to moan and kick her head back. The sensations from the ecstasy and sex are driving her to the edge of a second orgasm. As he fuels the orgasm about to explode inside of her, she starts driving his cock into her harder. "I want to feel it all the way up inside me," she moans.

"Oh fuck, I can feel it. I want you to come all over my cock."

"Oh God, I'm going to come!"

He feels her pussy pulsate around his cock. "Come on, Stac...come all over me!"

She lets off a loud scream. Her body starts convulses from the orgasm and she falls onto his chest. He slowly flips her onto her back. He slides his face down to her pussy and starts eating her out again. He puts her legs over his shoulders and slowly slides his cock into her super wet pussy.

"I want to feel you come, JJ," she moans. He starts pounding her pussy, pumping her with strong, powerful thrusts. He pushes her knees down into her chest. "Oh fuck, JJ...that feels so good! Fuck me just like that!"

He keeps pumping. "When I get ready to come, where do you want me to come?"

"Wherever you want, Baby. It's all about you now."

"Can I come in your mouth?"

"If that's what you want to do."

"When I get close, I'll tell you."

"Okay," she replies. He keeps pounding her and starts smacking her ass. "Yeah, just like that...keep going!"

"Oh shit," he pants. He can feel his cock start to pulsate. "I'm about to come!" He pulls out and tries to put his cock in her mouth. He doesn't make it far before blowing his load all over her face and into her mouth. "Oh my God," he moans.

She just giggles as the semen drips down her face onto her chest. She just grabs his cock and sucks on the head, trying to get every last drop he has left in his body.

"Fuck," he moans, as she sucks his cock.

"So how was that?" she asks.

"That was the most intense orgasm…the best I've ever had in my life. I'm definitely up for this all the time."

He moans as he rolls over onto his back on the bed.

"Well, maybe we'll just have to keep this going," she says as she smiles at him.

He returns her smile and sees his fresh orgasm covering her face. "Oh God, I'm sorry! Let me get you a towel!" He runs to his closet and grabs a towel. He hands it to her and lies back down on the bed.

"Thanks," she replies as she wipes off her face. "Hey, what time is it? Do you have a clock?"

"It's…wow, almost 5:00AM.," he replies.

"Are you serious? We've been messing around that long?"

"I guess time flies by when you're having fun."

"Yeah, that was definitely a lot of fun," she replies as she slides back into bed with him and rolls onto his chest.

They hear a knock on the door. "Hey, JJ?"

"Yeah, Mark?"

"Hey, me and Amy are going to Perkins. You and Stacy want to go?"

He looks at Stacy. "You want to go, Stacy?"

"No, I just want to lay here."

"Nah, we're good, Bro. You guys go ahead!"

"Hey, JJ?" Stacy asks.

"Yeah?"

"So, what's the deal with you selling this ecstasy stuff?"

# SMURF

A low ceiling of smoke and the smell of weed fill the game room of Smurf's house as he chills with a couple of buddies. The second half of the Bulls versus the Celtics passes across his thirty-two inch flatscreen, and another blunt is rolled. A large crash echoes throughout the house as the front door slams open.

"Shit, it's the police!" he yells as he runs toward the back door.

The police yell out remarks, but he pays no attention. His focus is on the back door.

*If I can just hit the door, I'm out of here.*

As he hits the back door, he gets tackled from the front by a waiting group of officers. "Stay down!" the lead officer yells.

"Fuck you!" he says in response.

"Oh, fuck me?" the officer responds and hits him in the back of his head with the butt of his gun.

"Stop resisting!" the officer yells as he hits him again.

He starts to go in and out of conscious as he continues to be beaten by the officers. After a few minutes of resisting, he finally gives in to the overpowering officers and is handcuffed. He's picked up and hauled to a squad car. "What am I being arrested for?"

The lead officer glares at him. "For the involvement in a triple homicide. Do you have anything to say?"

"I want my lawyer," he says and spits at the officer.

The officer hits him again, this time in the stomach. "Get this piece of shit out of my face."

While sitting in the intake pod in jail, a nasty urine-smelling place with one little sink in the corner and a shitty toilet that doesn't look to be working, he looks around the room, seeing all types of people--from people in for DUIs to guys looking to have been picked up while working the block, to junkies looking for another fix. He pushes his head against the wall.

*How did they find out? I killed all the witnesses. I watched them die. There is no way they could have talked. Did someone see my face?*

The anxiety of the unknown finally starts to tear him down. A correctional officer comes to the door. "Terrel Davis! Terrel Davis!

Smurf immediately comes out of his daydream. "Yeah?"

"You're Terrel Davis?"

"Yeah, I am."

"Alright, come with me."

He follows the officer into the processing room where he is

stripped, searched, and given jail clothing. His fingerprints are processed, and his mug shot is taken. The severity of the situation starts to set in.

*This is real... This shit is really happening! Smurf, don't show fear. Fear gets you into more trouble than it does anything.*

He is escorted to the D-block, where he is going to remain for the remainder of his time until his sentencing. He sits on his bunk and keeps replaying the night over and over in his head.

*No survivors. I know no one survived.*

"Davis, Terrel Davis!" the C.O. yells.

"What?" he responds.

"You got court, so go get ready."

He throws on his top and heads to the door. As he makes his way to the court hearing, a pit forms in his stomach. His anxiety is starting to get the best of him. As he stands next to the court-appointed pretender, the judge enters the courtroom and everyone stands.

"Everyone be seated," the judge says. "We're here today for the state of Illinois versus Terrel Davis. He is being charged with three counts of first degree murder, is that correct?"

"Yes, sir. That is correct." The prosecutor responds. He's a middle-aged white man in a pinstripe suit with short, brown hair. "We the people feel that he is dangerous to the community, Your Honor, and that he be held without bail."

The judge looks at the defense. "And you, Defense? Have anything to add?"

A man in his late forties with salt-and-pepper hair in a tailored three-piece suit stands. "Your Honor, my client has never been in trouble before this. He has family in town, so I don't feel he would be a flight risk. We ask that you set a bond for my client."

The judge nods. "I feel both ways on this matter, but the fact is that this is a case involving murder of another human being, and that needs to be looked at very seriously, so I will allow a bond, but I set it for three million dollars." He slams the mallet down.

Smurf looks at his lawyer. "Now what?"

"I'll meet with you tomorrow," he responds. "Just get back to the unit and relax and talk to no one, you understand me?" He nods and is escorted back to the jail.

Once in his cell, he lies in his bed and stares at the ceiling, wondering where this thing is going.

*I watched them die... I swear I did!*

He falls asleep, daydreaming the incident over and over again.

He's awoken the next day by a C.O. "Terrel Davis, you have a visitor."

As he leaves the unit, a million and one things are still running through his mind.

*How did they find out? How did they place me there? Who saw me leave?*

His lawyer stands as he enters the room. "Welcome, Mr. Davis. Have a seat."

He sits. "So what's it looking like?"

"Well, first, let me introduce myself. I'm Roger Penn, and I'll be representing you on this case. I'm doing this pro-bono, meaning that I'm actually a private attorney, but I'll be representing you free of charge. I've actually had some success with murder cases in my career, so I'm definitely going to represent you 100%, so if you have any questions? Don't be scared to ask, alright?"

After Smurf nods, Penn proceeds. "I've looked over the evidence, and in my opinion, I don't feel they even have a case. From what I see, they are basing all evidence on just two things. The first being only one witness who says they didn't get a good look at the shooter, but has a basic idea of what he looks like. Second, they said they saw a dark-colored SUV speed away from the apartment building. With that being said, do you have an alibi for that night? Do you own any SUV that could potentially match that description? See, what the state is going to try to do is place you at the scene by any means necessary, so we have to disprove the fact."

"Yeah, I understand," he replies. "I don't really have an alibi, but I don't own an SUV."

*At least not in my name…*

"So if they were to search records, no SUV will come back to your name?"

"No, sir."

"Okay," his lawyer responds. "Well, that's good for us. The state will also want to put you in a line-up for the witness, or they might do a photo-ray line up as of right now. I'm not sure, but from the looks of it, you have a very good chance of beating this, if you do all that I tell you to."

"What's that?" he replies.

"Just one thing. Do not, I repeat, do **not** talk to anyone about this and do not ever admit anything to me, because under law, I can't lie for you if I know the truth, alright? Do you have any questions, Terrel?"

"No sir, I don't."

"Okay. Well, just relax. I'm going to start pressing some issues to see what's going on with their end. If I hear any news on the case, I'll make sure to keep you posted either though mail or visits, alright? But just keep yourself busy and remember, talk to no one."

"Yes, sir," he replies. He shakes Roger's hand and exits the room.

*Man, this is going to be the longest year of my life!*

-----

The clicking from the doors wakes Smurf up. He soon remembers he's still in Cook County Jail. He swings his legs over the side of his bed and lets out a depressing sigh. "Fuck," he says to himself as he gets up and makes his way to the day room.

He hears some other inmates yell out, "On the new!" This meant a new person was on the unit. Smurf, a tall, young black male with cornrows in his hair, walks into the day room in his brown DOC-stamped shirt and pants. A few of the older guys walk up to him.

"What up, Youngster? Where you from?" one of them says.

"I'm from the Prinston Park area."

"Oh well, your guys are over there at the bottom tier," he says as he points to a group of guys standing on the bottom tier.

He makes his way over to the group and sees Jeff, one of his old partners from the street. Jeff recognizes him as soon as he looks up. "Yo, Smurf! What up, Cousin? What the fuck you doing?"

"Man, Jeff. They got me jammed up on some homicide shit," he replies.

"Damn, Family. That's messed up, but let me get you set up."

Jeff turns to the guy next to him and tells him to get a care kit. The guy takes off, and Jeff turns back to Smurf. "Smurf, is this your first bit?"

"Yeah, this is my first bit. I'm only twenty-one."

Jeff laughs. "Yeah, I forgot you're still a youngster. Since this is your first time down, let me give you rules to follow. First, if you need anything, talk to me. Don't fuck with any one of these offbrand niggas. If you got a problem with someone, holler at me because we stick together. One fights, we all fight, you feel me?"

"Yeah, I got you."

The guy returns with a care kit for him. "Here you go, Smurf," the guy says as he hands the package to him.

Jeff follows Smurf back to his cell. Smurf puts the package on his cot and turns to Jeff. "What the fuck you doing in here, anyway?"

Jeff leans against the wall. "You remember my baby mama, Carrie?"

"Yeah. What about her?"

"Me and that bitch got into it in front of her mama's house. She threw a brick through the front window on my new car, so I chased that bitch to her mama's house. She locked the door, so I kicked that fucking door in. Then I went in and fucked that bitch up. Her mama's bitch ass called police on me. Man, I hate that bitch anyway. I caught a domestic and a home invasion. But to make a long story short, me and my baby mama are still messing around, but her mama won't drop the home invasion charges. My baby mama didn't come to court on the domestic charges, so they threw it out. So, I'm fighting the home invasion charges, which carries six to thirty years, so I copped at the last court date to seven years, but they gave me the Buck Rogers court date so I don't go to sentencing for a while."

"So you said you just copped out the seven? Damn, how much time you got in all?"

"Man, I got eighteen months in by the time I go to court. I'll have...who knows...twenty in on seven? You have to do 50%, so three years, six months I'll have to do. So, I got like...another year and a half to two years left. All depends if I get halfway house house-arrest or work release. Then I'll be out sooner than that."

"True, true," he replies, shaking his head.

"So what up with your shit? Who they trying to say you killed?" Jeff asks with an interested look.

"Shit, Jeff. I don't know, man. All I know is that shit is crazy. Not only are they trying to put one murder on me, they're trying to put a triple homicide on me."

"A triple murder? That's some crazy ass shit, Family. So Smurf, what are you trying to be on while you are in here?"

"Jeff, I ain't on shit. Just chilling, trying to fight my case and stay sucker free, you feel me?"

"Yeah, I feel you," Jeff replies. "I will let you get settled in. If you need me, I'll be at the poker table."

"Alright, Fool. Let me get at you later," he says, pounding Jeff's fist. When Jeff leaves, Smurf sits down to evaluate the situation.

*Damn, I got a call my mama. I don't want to, but I got to. I know she's going to ask a bunch of questions.*

His cellmate enters, interrupting his thoughts. "What up, Cousin?" he says. "I'm Dre. What's your name?"

"Everyone calls me Smurf."

"For you to know which is yours. That your commissary box down there," he says as he points down to a gray box. He then points to a shelf and says, "That shelf is yours."

"The only rules I have for this room is be respectful. Don't touch nothing that doesn't belong to you. Same rules that apply to you also apply to me. If you take a shit, put the towel up, and if you drop one, flush. I got some books and magazines down there by the desk," he says as he points to the stack of books and magazines. "Besides that, everything should be cool."

Smurf nods his head in agreement. The C.O. yells out, "Chow time! Chow time!"

Jeff comes up to the door, "Hey, Family. You going?"

"No, I'm good," he replies.

"Well, let me get your tray if you're not gonna eat."

"Okay, I got you."

Before they leave, Jeff looks over at Dre. "Don't be fucking with my man Smurf either, Dre." Dre just smiles and laughs.

On their way to the line, Jeff says, "Your celly is a very cool guy, and all he wants is respect, so y'all should get along."

Once in line, Smurf sees the trays of food that one of the guys carries past. He looks at Jeff.

"What the fuck is that?"

Jeff laughs. "Mystery meat and mashed potatoes."

"Why'd you call it mystery meal?"

"Because we don't know what the fuck it is," Jeff says.

"So you can have everything but the apple," he says, picking up his tray.

"Alright, cool," Jeff replies. "So what are you going to do?"

"I'm going to go lay down. I got too much shit on my mind."

"Alright, Family. I got a stress reliever for you, so holler at me after count, alright?"

After eating, he heads back to his room and lies down to relax. Count time comes and passes. He gets up and makes his way down to

Jeff's room.

"So what is a stress reliever in here, Fool?"

"Workout," he responds.

Smurf gives him a funny look. "Workout?"

"Yes, workout Nigga."

"Jeff, I don't need to work out. I already have a banging ass body."

"Whatever, Nigga. Come on, let's go work out."

The two work out until it's close to dinnertime. After dinner, he finds a seat in front of the TV.

*Should I call my mom? You know what? Fuck it*, he thinks and heads to the phones.

As he starts dialing the phone number, all he can do is think about what his mom is going to say. The phone starts ringing. He gets the nervous shakes. He tries to hold them back, but it's hard. This is his mother. The one woman that means the world to him. He sits, waiting for his mom to answer. He starts sweating a little as he continues to think of what she's going to say. She finally answers.

"Hello?"

The phone operator comes over the earpiece. "You have a collect call from …"

"Terrel," he says into the phone.

"… an inmate at Cook County Jail," the operator continues. "To accept, press one. To reject, press five."

The sound of a button being pushed takes what feels like a million pounds off his chest.

"Hello, Terrel Honey," his mom says.

*What a sweet sounding voice it is to hear...* "Hi Mom," he responds.

"Oh my God, Terrel! What happened to you? I haven't talked to you in a few days! Are you okay? What did you do now?"

"Mom, this is hard to explain, but they arrested me on a triple homicide case."

"They did what?!" she yells into the phone. "You did what?! Are you crazy?! A murder, Terrel?!"

"Mom, Mom, relax. I didn't do it. They got the wrong person," he says. He can hear his mom crying on the other end.

"Where did I go wrong? I did everything a single parent could to try and keep you off those streets. I kept taking you to church to keep you in a positive atmosphere. I had lots of great hopes for you, Terrel. I really hope you didn't do what they said you did."

"Mom, I told you I didn't do it! They got the wrong guy. You don't believe your own son?"

"Don't you raise your voice to me. I'm your mother. I'm fifty-two years old... I taught you to respect your elders."

"Yes, you did. I'm sorry, Mom. I'm just stressed out with this whole situation."

"That you are, but you're doing okay though, right?" she asks with concern in her voice.

"Some guys helped me out when I got here. Since I didn't have any money, they gave me shampoo, toothpaste, shower shoes and..."

His mom cuts him off. "Do you need money?"

"I hate to ask, but can you send me some, please?"

"I'll send you some money. Okay, Honey?"

"All right, thank you, Mom," he says, sounding a little more uplifted.

"Terrel, do they have visitation down there?"

"Yeah, they do. It's on the weekends...from 9:00am to 3:00pm and 4:00pm to 8:00pm."

"Okay...well, I'm going to try and make it down there to see you, okay?"

"If you want, you can come. I don't really want you to see me like this, but I can't stop you. But Mom, I'm going to let you go though, okay?

"Alright, Honey. I love you, Terrel. Keep your head up. I believe God will fix this problem and help you son," his mom says with encouragement.

"I love you too, Mom. I hope He does, too. Bye, Mom."

"Goodbye," his mom responds, then hangs up.

He puts the receiver back in its cradle and takes a few deep breaths.

*Well, that didn't go as bad as I thought... shit, there ain't shit to do.... I guess I'll head to my room and relax for a while.*

As he lies in his bed and stares at his ceiling, the only thing he can do is think about that crazy night.

*I swear, no one survived those gunshots. No one saw me--or maybe someone did see me with Robbie...but I swear it, no one saw me!*

He plays the scene over and over in his mind.

*From Smoke's apartment... Bang, one to the head. Bang, one to the head. They both died. I watched them. But then there was Smoke's wife... But I hit her in the leg with that random shot, then unloaded one more into her head. Maybe someone saw me kill her...but then I ran for the door. I do remember hearing a door open behind me, so I fired that random shot off. Maybe the person saw me kill her, but there's no way they saw my face... I never faced that direction. Am I forgetting something? All I know is that my lawyer better be good. My life is at stake with this shit, and I ain't going down without a fight.*

He lays in a semi-trance on his bed. He wakes up fast to a bang on the door. It's Jeff. "What are you doing? Get your ass up, man!"

"Jeff, I'm tired."

"Are you going to lay down for the rest of the day?"

"I don't know...maybe."

"Alright, you lazy fuck. Get some rest. If you want to come out, I'll be at the poker table. All right, Smurf?"

"Alright, Jeff. I'll see you in a bit."

As Jeff leaves, he rolls over and looks up at the ceiling again.

*Man, when I get out of this, I'm gonna kill that nigga Yeo.*

Bliss

# JJ

The vibrating of JJ's phone wakes him as he lies in bed with Stacy's head on his chest. He slowly opens his eyes and looks around.

"Ugh," he mumbles as he tries to brace her head and slowly move it without waking her. He's tired from sleep and is moving sluggishly. His phone isn't on his bedside table like it normally is.

"Where the hell is that thing?" he says, crawling on the ground. "Finally," he says as he reaches into his pants pocket. His fingers touch more than his phone. He pulls everything out from his pocket.

He's staring at a large stack of money.

*What the hell is all this?*

He's looking at the money when his phone begins to vibrate again. It's a text from Leon.

Hey, J. I hope last night went good for you. Call me or stop by later. I'll be home chillin.

JJ closes the phone and tosses it on to the ground. He puts the money in the drawer on his computer desk and climbs back into bed.

He goes back to sleep for another few hours, but this time he wakes up to a pair of soft hands sliding slowly up and down his stomach. He looks down to see Stacy staring at him.

"Good morning," she whispers.

"Good morning," he replies, still sounding tired. "Did you have fun last night?"

"I had a great time. Probably one of the best nights since I've been in college. What about you? Did you have fun?"

"Yeah, I had a lot of fun. I definitely didn't think me and you would be here right now, though."

She yawns. "Why do you say that?"

"Well, I mean...I didn't know you were going to be out last night...and I definitely didn't think you would pop a pill with me. When you did, it totally blew my mind."

"You don't think of me differently, do you?"

"Oh God, no! I'm happy you trust me enough to try it with me." She snuggles up closer to him, and he smiles. "I don't know if you know this, but I've had a crush on you for a while."

She looks up and smiles. "Well, I have a secret, too. I've liked you for a while, but thought that you doing drugs was kind of a turn off...but after last night, I know why you do what you do, and I can't knock you for doing that. I will admit, I really enjoyed last night. That ecstasy stuff really just made everything feel great. I know why everyone likes it so much now. The sounds the music made were so beautiful...and the colors were so full and intense." She pauses. "Hey, what time is it by the way?"

He checks his phone. "My clock says it's almost 1:00."

"Are you serious? I got class at 2:30! Shit...I need to get to my house and get ready for class. Can you run me home?"

"Yeah, no big deal."

They dress and walk into the living room. "Do you have everything?" he asks.

"Yeah," she responds. "I wonder how Amy is doing."

He grabs his keys off the kitchen bar. "I bet sleeping."

After a short drive, they are in front of her apartment. "That's my apartment building right there," she says, pointing to a small complex on their right.

He slows to a stop. "Hope you have a good day in class."

"Yeah, me too. I have a lecture to go to, so lots of notes," she replies before getting out of the car. She turns to him, leans in, and kisses him.

He smiles. "What's that for?"

"For last night," she says. She leans in and kisses him again. "And this will make you want to call me later."

"If that's what you want, it definitely worked," he says with a big smile on his face.

-----

He returns home and remembers the text that Leon had sent him. He takes the money from his desk drawer and throws it on the bed. He starts counting until he reaches $400, the amount he owes his cousin. He puts it off to the side.

*Man, I still got a lot of money sitting here.*

He continues to count the cash. This time he counts up to $1,100.

*Damn, that's crazy! I just made a thousand dollars in one night! If I can do this twice a week, I can average $2,000 a week or $8,000 a month... I would be able to pay off school before I even finished it!*

He laughs and picks up his phone to text Leon.

**Hey cousin, are you at home? I want to tell you about last night too.**

He sends the text, then gets up to hop in the shower. After he's changed, his phone rings from a text from Leon.

Hey J. I'm home. Stop by when you can.

JJ responds with a text saying he'll be there within thirty minutes. He grabs the money he owes Leon and some extra to buy another hundred pills and heads to Leon's.

He knocks on the door when he gets there.

"Come on in! It's unlocked!" Leon yells from inside. He enters the apartment and closes the door behind him. "Lock it! Yo J, want a soda?" Leon yells from the kitchen.

"Yeah, please." He walks over and sits down on the chair in the living room. Leon comes out carrying two sodas and hands one to him. "Thanks, Leon."

"So J, tell me how last night was."

"It was a blast! I haven't had that much fun in a while. I saw my friend Stacy at the club and got her and her friend to pop pills with us.

We ended up taking them home and fucking them."

"Shit, sounds like a pretty damn good night! So how did the selling go?"

JJ reaches into his pocket and puts Leon's $400 on the table. "That's the money I owe you."

"Damn, you sold them all!" Leon says. He grabs the cash and puts in his pocket.

JJ pulls out another $400 and puts it on the table. "I need another jar."

Leon nods his head. "Alright, gimme a second." He leaves the room and returns with a baggie full of one hundred ten pills and tosses them to him.

"Thank you," JJ replies. "But yeah, last night was crazy. I gave Mark the pills, and he ended up coming back with all the money early in the night."

"See, J? Look at how easy it is to make money. You didn't even do anything at the club and probably made $1,000 last night, huh?"

JJ laughs. "Yeah, pretty close to that. Hopefully Mark can do what he did last night, and I'll make more cash tonight. I don't think I'm going to go out tonight though, so we'll see what happens."

"That's cool. Just let me know if you need more. Text me when you want to stop by, and I'll let you know what's up. You know me and cell phones. I don't like talking about stuff on them."

"Okay."

"Want to smoke?"

"Nah, I'm okay. I gotta get going and find Mark...let him know what's going on."

"Alright. If you need me, just text."

JJ goes back to his apartment and finds Mark chilling on the living room couch. "Yo, Mark. How are you feeling today?"

"Actually man, those pills are pretty damn clean! I don't feel bad at all! Actually, I felt pretty good!"

"How was last night with Amy?"

"She was pretty good," he says, laughing. "Bro, you wouldn't believe me if I even told you. Let's just say she is the most flexible girl I've ever messed with...and she had one of the best pussies ever! What about you and Stacy? You've had a thing for her for years."

"She has the most perfect tits I've ever seen! And man, that girl can give head like a pro. She could suck rust off a chrome bumper...she could definitely do it. I almost busted before we even had sex. She told me to call her later today...but Mark, you wouldn't believe it! She told me she's had a thing for me about as long as I have for her." He pauses. "Did you put the money away that you made last night, by the way?"

"Yeah, I can't believe I made $500 that fast! I would love to do that all the time. I might be able to save and open a business when I get out of college."

JJ pulls out the new baggie of pills and puts them on the table. "So you think you're up for working tonight?"

Excitement fills Mark's face. "Damn, you got another one hundred ten pills?... I don't know if I could sell them all tonight, though."

"I'll tell you what...I'll give you the one hundred pills for $1,000. Just do what you did last night, twice a week. That's $2,000 a week, $8,000 a month, and $96,000 a year. I bet that's enough to help you start your business."

"Hell yeah! I can definitely open my business with that, but I don't know if I could do all one hundred tonight."

"It's cool if you don't. Try on Saturday night... just try to get me the cash by Sunday."

Mark picks up the pills and walks off to his room. JJ picks up his cell and calls his parent's house. A sweet sounding female voice says hello.

"Hi, Mom. What are you doing?"

"Oh, JJ! Hi, honey! I'm not doing anything, just cleaning the house. What's going on with you in school? Are you ready for Spring Break? Are you still coming home then?"

"Well, that's why I'm calling. I was going to come home, but I don't think I'll have time. Some of the guys want to do something, so I'm just going to stay here."

"Oh, really?" his mom says, sounding a little sad. "Well, I guess if that's what you want to do, that's fine. Maybe this summer then."

"Yeah, what about the Fourth of July?"

"Okay, Honey. That sounds good. Dad's here. Hold on; I'll get him. I love you."

"I love you, too."

His dad grabs the phone. "Hello?" the familiar deep voice says.

"Hi, Dad."

"How's school? How are you doing on money? Do you need any?"

"No, I'm good for now, thanks...but hey, I got to get going. I just wanted to call and tell you guys I love you and miss you."

"We love you, too. Be safe, okay?"

"I will. Talk to you later," he replies, then presses END. He sits back in the chair, thinking about Stacy. Not wanting to seem desperate, he decides not to call. *Just wait it out...*

------

The day turns into night, and he's still waiting for her to call or text. He sits on his computer, researching chemical compounds. He looks up at the poster of Alexander Shulgin, the father of ecstasy.

*I want to be like you... I want to create a new drug to change this world forever.*

"JJ, are you in there?" Mark's voice echoes through the door.

"Yeah, come in."

Mark enters the room. "Hey J, are you going out tonight?"

"No, I'm staying in. I'm waiting for Stacy to call. Who are you going with?"

"I called Amy and we're going back to Club E. Looks like I found a new party girl...thanks, JJ!"

He just smiles. "No problem. You and Amy have fun. Just remember the cash."

"No worries, Bro. Work first, play later. I'll see you later," Mark says as he closes the door.

JJ turns back around to continue his research on legal and illegal drugs. His phone vibrates on the desk. He flips it open. It's a text from Stacy.

Hi JJ I just woke up from my day of school and work I wanted to see if you want to hang out if you're not busy but if you are that's cool too.

**Hey Stacy I'm just chilling at home you want to come over?**

As he waits for a reply, he goes back to researching. The reply comes back in a matter of minutes.

Sure I'll come hang out. I'll be over in an hour or so. See you then.

**OK see you soon.**

He puts down the phone, goes back to his computer and saves his research to the hidden folder on his computer. He hurries to shower and get dressed before Stacy gets there. He's zipping his pants when he hears a knock on the front door.

"Just one second!" he yells. He grabs a shirt from his dresser and goes to the door. The door swings open, and Stacy is standing in the doorway, dressed in a pair of blue jeans, a dark red hoodie with white fur on the inner part of the hood, and a pair of dark red UGG boots.

She smiles when she sees him. "Hey, JJ."

He gives her a quick kiss and gestures to the couch. "Are you thirsty?" He slips his shirt on as he walks to the fridge.

"No, I'm fine, thanks," she replies as she sits on the couch and takes off her hoodie, revealing a tight, white T-shirt.

He makes his way to the couch and sits down. "So what's up? School go okay for you today?"

"It was okay. I was still tired from last night, so when I got home, I fell asleep... I would've gotten a hold of you earlier. You didn't go out with Mark tonight?"

"I didn't want to go out tonight...plus, he's got his new party buddy, Amy," he says, laughing.

Stacy smiles. "That's cool. They would make a very cute couple. So what do you want to do tonight?"

"I don't care, just watch a movie, maybe. What do you want to do?"

"I don't care. We can watch a movie if you want."

"Yeah, let's do that," he says. He gets up, grabs a movie from the shelf and puts it in.

Before too long, they end up in his room. At first they start making out, feeling all over each other. He slides his fingers through her hair, down her chest and her legs.

"No sex this time," she says. "Will you just lay with me?"

He agrees. He hangs his hands over her waist and falls asleep. He wakes up to his name being called through the door. It's Mark. He slowly gets out of bed, trying not to wake Stacy, and heads toward the living room. Mark and Amy are sitting on the couch, watching TV.

"What's up, Mark?" he says. "Hi, Amy." He sits down in the chair. "How's tonight?"

Mark pulls out a wad of money and hands it to him. "It's all there."

"Are you kidding me?" he asks in disbelief.

"All of it! Yeah, bro! You got yourself a moneymaker there, JJ.

Everyone wants it!"

He counts the cash; all $1,000 is there. "Damn, Mark! You didn't do too bad then, huh?"

Mark looks at him and smiles. "Yeah, not too bad." Mark hints at him to go back to his room.

JJ follows his cue "Well guys, I'm beat. Thanks again, Mark. Nice to see you again, Amy. You guys have a good night."

They say their goodnights and he heads back to his room. He places the money in a shoebox with the money he made the day before. He climbs back into bed with Stacy, but this time he lies on his back, facing the ceiling.

*Man, this is crazy how easy it is to make money.*

# SMURF

A few months pass, and Smurf is wondering about the status of his case. He still hasn't heard from his lawyer. He decides to call his lawyer's office. The secretary answers. "Hello. Thank you for calling Penn and Johnson Law Firm. How can I help you?"

"Yeah, I'm wanting to talk to Roger Penn," Smurf says.

"I'm sorry Sir, but he's out of the office at the moment. Do you want me to connect you to his voicemail?"

"No, I'm looking for someone that can help me get information about my case."

"What is your name, Sir?"

"It's Terrel Davis."

"Hold on one minute. I'll check and see if I can find someone to help you." After a few minutes, she comes back to the phone. "Mr. Davis?"

"Yeah."

"I don't have any information, but I do know you're scheduled to be seen by Mr. Penn in the next few weeks."

"Alright. I guess I'll wait," he says as he hangs up in anger.

"Man, I fucking hate wasting my time with these fucking lawyers!"

Seeing this reaction, Jeff walks over. "What's up, Fam? You good?"

"Nah, I just got off the phone with my lawyer's secretary. These fuckers are giving me the run around."

"Well, first thing you gotta do Smurf is relax. You got to let them lawyers do their jobs, but stay on them at the same time. Plus Fmily, you're facing a triple murder. You got to relax. This is our time to work out, so forget that shit and let's go work out."

They begin their normal routines on the machines. "So, you messing with any bitches out there?" Jeff asks.

"Nah...mess with a chick here and there, but nothing serious. I was about getting money when I was out there. Why, what's up?"

"Well, I wanna get your mind off this case. I'm gonna holler at my girl today and see if she can find you someone to communicate with...keep your ass grounded, or you're gonna drive yourself crazy in here."

As they're finishing up their workout, the C.O. yells, "Lunch!"

Smurf walks over and picks up his tray. "Man, this shit is nasty," he says under his breath. "I can't believe I'm eating this shit. Only good shit on this tray is the cookies. Bullshit white rice, nasty ass chicken."

He takes his cookies and makes his way back to his room. He passes the next few hours watching TV until he hears the C.O yell for count. He goes back to his room and lies down to take a nap until dinner. As soon as he feels his eyes close, he hears a loud thump against his door. He jumps up in a frantic jolt.

*What the fuck?*

He looks around to see Jeff at the door. "Come on, man. It's about to be dinnertime."

With his mind still trying to catch up to his body after a deep sleep, Smurf moves sluggishly to get down from his bed and heads out to the tables. They get their trays and sit down at a table.

"Hey Fam, I talked to my girl Tanya today... She said she talked about you to a friend of hers. She said the girl's name was Courtney, and she was interested...supposed to let you know to hit her up."

"I'll hit her up. I need me a bitch to keep my mind going, because if I don't, this case is going to drive me crazy."

They talk for another hour. Eventually Smurf says, "Jeff, I'm going back to bed Fam. I'm beat."

"Ight, Smurf. I'll hit you up in a little bit."

"Davis, Terrel Davis," the C.O. calls out.

It's mail call, and he is surprised to hear his name called out. He feels like a kid finding Christmas presents under the tree on Christmas morning.

*I wonder who sent me mail?*

He grabs the letter from the C.O. It's from his mother. He heads back to his cell and begins to read the letter.

"Dear Terrel,

I hope this letter helps put you in good spirits. I know you're facing a hard time in your life and that you probably feel alone, but just know I'm here with you and for you. You're my son and will always be my son. Don't you forget that. Every day you're in my prayers that God will bring you home to me. Keep your head up and stay positive. You're in a very negative place, so keep pushing forward and it will be all right. Also, I sent you $100 to help you buy shampoo and necessities and so you can get some snacks, too. I bet that food isn't like what I cook, huh? I hope that made you laugh. Well Terrel, I'm going to get going–I got something at the church tonight, so I'll talk to you soon. Call if you want or if you need anything.

I love you so much!

Your Mom"


He takes a couple deep breaths and smiles. He's amazed how such a small thing like getting a piece of mail can bring such happiness to a person. He folds the letter and puts it back in the envelope before placing it under his mattress. Still a bit surprised, he heads to find Jeff. He finds him watching TV.

"Yo Jeff, what's up? How's this commissary shit work around here?"

"Well, you gotta go get a list and fill it out and hand it in. Then they will bring it to you. Make sure you check it, though. These bitches are good at charging you and not giving you all your shit."

"Yeah, my mom sent some money to help me out a little bit."

"That's good that you got a few people willing to help you out while you're gone. All these nigga's in here, most of them burned their

bridges when they were out...now they are barely surviving."

"I guess I don't have it as bad as I thought."

"Yeah, there is always someone that has it worse than you.

Remember that."

The night rolls into the next day. He's watching TV when a C.O.

calls out his name. "Terrel Davis!"

"What's up?" he yells.

"You got a visitor, so get ready."

"Who is it?" he yells back. "I'm not expecting anyone."

"Well, someone is here to see you," the C.O. replies and walks

away.

He heads back to his room, gets dressed, and heads to the visitor's

area. He starts to get nervous, thinking it could be his lawyer. He gets

into the visiting room, and to his surprise, he finds a sexy, dark skin Nia

Long look-a-like with short hair, waiting on the other side of the glass.

*Damn!*

"Hey, Terrel," the girl says. "I'm Courtney. I'm a friend of

Tanya's...Jeff's girl. She told me I might be interested in one of Jeff's friends. I asked her who it was, and Tanya said it was a guy they call Smurf on the streets, but his real name is Terrel Davis. I told her 'Oh my God! I went to school with him!'"

Still in a state of shock and confusion; he can't put the name with the face.

She sees this and laughs. "I used to go to school with you in junior high. I used to be chubby, with braces and long curly hair. You and your friends used to make fun of me and call me names."

He still looks at her with a blank stare.

"You guys used to call me 'Jaws' because of my braces."

Recognition flickers in his mind, and he leans in toward the glass window. "Courtney Dalion? Is that you?"

A huge smile instantly appears on her face and she giggles. "Yeah, it's me."

"Damn girl, you've changed a lot!"

She smiles. "Yeah, I cut my hair short, got my braces off, and grew into my body.

He smiles. "Well, I'm sorry for making fun of you back in school."

"It's okay, just kids being kids. That's in the past. I see you haven't changed too much, Terrel. Just gotten older."

He laughs. "And you've changed a lot!"

"You know what's crazy, Terrel? Back in school, I had the biggest crush on you, but you never gave me the time of day. I understand I wasn't very good looking back then."

He stays quiet. She smiles.

"At a loss for words?"

He lets out a cough. "You gotta have all the guys chasing you now, huh?"

"Well, let's just say they chase, but I don't pay them no attention. It's my turn to do what the boys did to me when we were young."

"Damn, this some payback shit? You just getting back at me for when we were young and dumb?"

"Nah, I really wanted to see you."

Unsure of what to say, he changes the subject. "So, what are you doing now these days then, Courtney?"

"Well, I'm doing school still, but I'm almost finished with my college degree in fashion design and marketing. A local company here in the city wants to hire me on full time after I graduate. I work there part time now. What about you, Terrel? What did you do to get put in here?"

"They are trying to accuse me of doing something I didn't do, so I'm fighting these people. I don't really want to talk about it...for real, Courtney."

"Oh, I'm sorry...no problem...we'll talk about something else." Courtney looks down at her watch. "It's almost time to go. Do you want me to come back and visit you?"

"Yeah, whenever you're free. It was really good seeing you. Thanks for coming. You don't understand how it feels to get a visit from the outside world. Plus, once you're out of sight, you're out of mind with everyone. I've only got one letter from my mother and one visit from you since I came to jail. It makes you wonder where everybody's heads are at."

"I know we haven't talked for a good amount of time, but I'm here for you. I'll try to stop back again soon, alright? Just keep busy. I'll see you later, Terrel."

"I'll see you soon," he says before standing. He gets escorted back to the unit.

*Man, Courtney looked bad...and that pearly white smile...man, it's to die for!*

As the next few days pass, his mind stays occupied with the normal day activities and thoughts about his situation. He's watching TV, waiting for Jeff to come around for their daily workout, when he hears the C.O. yell his name for mail call. Surprised, he grabs the letter. It's from Courtney. He goes back to his cell to read the letter.

*"Dear Terrel,*

*I sent this letter to say hello and to brighten your day. I've been thinking about you a lot since our visit. I enjoyed it a lot, and I hope you really did too! I'm planning to come visit in a few days after you receive this letter. Also, I put $50 on your account with this letter. I know that's not much, but it helps in case you need food or hygiene items. Well, I'm going to get going. I'll see you soon.*

*Courtney"*

He folds up the letter and goes to put it back into the envelope, but sees another piece of paper. He pulls it out and unfolds it. It's the receipt for the $50 she sent. He smiles and places both sheets of paper back into the envelope and places them under his mattress.

He goes to look for Jeff and finds him in his usual spot by the TV.

"Yo Jeff, what up, Family?"

"What's up, Smurf? I heard your name get called. Who wrote you?"

"I got mail from Courtney, the girl that your chick hooked me up with."

"Damn, Family! First a visit, now a letter... What is this love connection shit?" Jeff says, laughing.

He laughs. "It's no love connection shit, but I just see it like this...it is what it is. She said she's going to come visit again in a few days. She even put some cash on my books, too."

"Good to hear. Tanya hooked you up with a cool bitch."

"Tell Tanya I say thanks too, Family."

"No problem, Smurf. I got you."

As they sit talking, another inmate in the unit yells, "On the new!"

They both look toward the door as two new guys walk in. He gets a sick feeling that he knows them, but he can't figure out where from.

As they come closer, his body starts to go numb. Jeff looks at him. "What the fuck's up? You know them niggas?"

"Yeah, I know them niggas. Them little ass niggas jumped me before I came to jail."

Jeff looks at the two guys, then back to Smurf. "You sure it's them?"

"Fuck yeah, Jeff. I remember seeing one of their faces, so fuck them both!" He hops up and heads toward the two guys.

*These little ass niggas will be my message to Smoke's son. I'm gonna whoop that little nigga's ass when I get out of here, too.*

He takes a deep breath, his hand cocked into a fist by his side. He looks at the guy on the right.

"Yo, little nigga. Your ass ain't protected in here."

# JJ

A touch of warm skin and the sound of a beating heart wake JJ. He notices his face nestled perfectly on Stacy's breasts. He looks to see if she is awake, but she is still sound asleep.

He gets up slowly, so as not to wake her, and opens his closet. He reaches in the back and pulls out the shoebox. He looks back at Stacy one more time to make sure she is sleeping and opens up the top of the box. Inside are five large stacks of cash and a baggie of red, blue, and green ecstasy pills. These are his gains from a month's worth of selling. The pills are a hit on the college campus, and he is raking in the money. The business acts like a revolving door - the drugs come in, Mark takes them out, then the money comes back.

*It's almost too easy...*

Stacy begins to moan and move around in the bed. "Oh shit," he says. He places the box back inside his closet.

"Honey?" her sweet voice says. "What are you doing?"

"Oh, nothing. I was just looking in my closet for something. Nothing special, though."

"Come back to bed."

He climbs back in and snuggles under the blankets.

"Can you believe we've been seeing each other for three months now?" she asks, rubbing her hands over his chest.

"I can't believe we've been dating for as long as we have. I still remember the first night we got together, like it was yesterday," he replies. He kisses her neck softly. The romantic moment is interrupted by his cell phone.

He reaches for his phone, but she touches his arm. "Just let it ring. Come back to bed."

He looks back at her. "I can't. It could be important." He grabs his cell. "Hello?"

"What are you doing?" he hears Mark ask.

"Nothing, just chilling with Stacy. What's up?"

"I wanted to see if you could give me a ride somewhere right now. The sooner the better."

"Do I just need to drop you off?"

"I just need a ride over to my buddy's place."

"Okay, where are you at now?"

"I'm at the gas station by our place."

"Okay, I'll be there in ten minutes."

"Okay, I'll see you soon."

JJ presses END and looks at Stacy. "That was Mark. He needs a ride."

"Okay," she says and smiles. "Let's go get him, drop him off, and go get some food. I'm starving."

"Alright."

Right before they walk out the door, he stops. "Hold on one second. I forgot something in my room."

He goes back to his room, opens up his closet door and grabs $300 out of the shoebox. They leave the apartment and head to the gas station. Mark is standing outside. Stacy hops out to let Mark ride up front.

"Thanks," Mark says as he gets in.

"Where's your car, Mark?" Stacy asks.

"Man, I let Amy use it and she's busy, but I needed to get over to this guy's house because I'm meeting someone about trying to get them to buy some pills."

"Oh, how are you doing?" JJ asks.

"I got my personal left. I will get more from you tonight."

"Alright. Well Stacy and I are going to go eat after dropping you off, so we can meet later."

"Yeah, that's fine. Turn right up there, and it's the blue house."

JJ parks the car in the driveway, and Mark hops out. "Stacy, it's always a pleasure," Mark says. "I'll call you later, JJ."

Mark leaves, and Stacy climbs back into the front seat. "So where do you want to go to eat?" JJ asks.

"I'm kind of hungry for steak. How about Hickory Park?"

"Yeah, that sounds good."

They pull into the restaurant parking lot. "What do you want to do tonight?" Stacy asks as they get out of the car.

"I don't care. You want to go to the club again?"

"Yeah, we can go and just hang out for a while, maybe have a few drinks."

"Yeah, I just want to chill." He looks at the crowd outside the restaurant. "Man Stacy, this place is packed! I swear everybody in town loves this place. Maybe because you're able to watch them cook the food, and it's all homemade."

"Yeah, I bet this is the best food in town," Stacy agrees.

JJ opens the front door, letting Stacy walk in first. They walk up to the front desk, where a young lady dressed in blue jeans and a black T-shirt is standing.

"Hello, welcome to Hickory Park. Our wait right now is about twenty minutes. Would you like me to put your name on the list?" she asks.

"Yeah, go ahead and put our name down."

"Okay sir. What is your last name?"

"Smith."

"Okay, Mr. Smith. We will call your name over the loudspeaker when your table's ready."

"Okay, thank you."

He and Stacy walk back through the front door to wait outside. Stacy turns to him. "JJ, your last name isn't Smith."

He chuckles. "Yeah, my dad did that a lot in Chicago. People couldn't say our last name, so he just started saying Smith."

Stacy laughs. "Your dad is pretty smart."

"Yeah, he's good at what he does. He is definitely no dummy, that's for sure."

The two of them wait for about fifteen minutes before they hear, "Smith, party of two," repeated three times over the loudspeaker.

"That's us. Let's go," JJ says.

They make their way back into the front lobby. The young lady is standing at the counter with two menus in her hands. "Mr. Smith, follow me please," she says. JJ follows Stacy and the hostess through the packed restaurant to a corner table that allows diners to overlook the rest of the dining area.

"I really like this booth," he says as he sits down.

"You really do have a good view from here," Stacy agrees.

"I think I'm going to get the barbecue cheeseburger, fries and a shake. What about you? What do you want?"

"I really want a steak, but that's kind of expensive."

"Don't worry about the price. I got it. Just get what you want."

"I really want to get a New York strip steak with baked potato and a salad."

"Okay then, we're ready to order."

They order, and the waitress leaves. JJ pulls his phone from his pocket and places it on the table. "Come on, JJ. Do you really have to put that on table?"

"What do you mean?"

"We are getting ready to eat. Can we just have one dinner without you messing with your cell phone?"

He just shrugs it off and places the phone to the side. A few minutes go by then his phone begins to vibrate. Stacy glares at him. "Oh, stop that shit, Stacy. It's just a text message."

He flips open his phone to see a message from Mark.

Hey dude, I need to meet up now. I'm going to be very busy tonight.

He calls Mark and Mark answers after the first ring. "Dude, where are you at? I need to see you."

"Mark, I'm busy with Stacy. We are eating dinner. Can't this wait 'til we're done?"

"No, I'm trying to get this done ASAP."

"Where are you?"

"I'm at home."

"Alright, go into my room, and go into my closet."

"Okay, I'm in here." He can hear shuffling on the other end.

"Alright, see that blue-and-white box?"

"The shoebox?"

"Open it."

More shuffling. "Oh shit, jackpot!" Marks says, laughing.

"Shut up Mark, and grab the baggy."

"Okay, how many concert tickets are here?"

"one-hundred-fifty."

"Okay, I got you later tonight. Are you guys going to the club later?"

"Yeah, we will be there."

"Okay, we'll talk there."

"That's cool. Me and Stacy will see you later," he replies, then presses END He turns it off and places it in his pocket. "Now we won't be bothered for the rest of the night."

"Whatever JJ, you live on that thing," she replies.

"Well, it did just buy us dinner and alcohol tonight."

"Yeah, I guess," she replies in an irritated voice.

The food arrives and they spend the next twenty minutes eating. They finish, and he reaches for his phone and turns it back on. "So Stacy, back to my place so we can get ready for tonight?"

"Yeah, but can we stop by my place so I can run in and grab some jeans and a shirt?

"Yeah, we can go there first and then head to my place so we can chill and get ready."

The server returns with the check. "Let me know when you're ready to pay."

JJ reaches into his pocket and pulls out the wad of money, but Stacy grabs the check first.

"Damn!" she says in amazement.

"What is it?"

"The bill is $80."

He counts out five $20 bills. "Here you go," he says, handing it to the waiter.

"Do you need change, Sir?"

"No, it's all yours."

As the server counts the money, he looks at JJ. "Excuse me, Sir, but you might have made a mistake. You gave me a $20 tip."

JJ smiles and shakes his head. "It's no mistake. You did a great job. Great work deserves great pay."

"Well thank you, Sir! You two have a great night!"

They leave the restaurant and head toward Stacy's house. He slows down once they get close and puts the car in park. She gets out and returns a few minutes later with a bag of clothes.

"Hold on a sec," he says. "I'm going to call Jimmy and let him know we're coming tonight."

She nods, and he calls Jimmy.

"Hello," the familiar voice says over the phone.

"Hey, Jimmy. It's JJ."

"Hey, what's up?"

"Stacy and I are coming out tonight. We need a V.I.P table and a couple of bottles."

"Okay, what do you want?"

"Can you get me two bottles of Grey Goose?"

"Yeah, not a problem. Is Mark going to be coming with you?"

"Yeah, we are going to meet him there."

"Okay, sounds good. He sent me a text earlier, so I didn't know, but yeah, I will be at the door tonight and I'll make sure you guys get in."

"Sounds good, thanks."

He hangs up and drives back to his apartment. Once inside, Stacy heads for the shower, while he decides to sit on his bed and do more research. His phone vibrates with a text from Mark.

Hey man we still good for tonight?

**Yeah. I'll see you at the club. I'm busy right now.**

He presses SEND, then hops in the shower while Stacy gets dressed in his room. He returns to find Stacy still half naked in skintight jeans.

"Wow, look at you," he says with a smile.

She turns and looks at him. He walks over to the backside of her and wraps his arms around her stomach and begins kissing her neck softly. She reaches her arms up and grabs onto the back of his neck. She lets off a soft moan as she turns around and pushes him onto his bed. She climbs on top of him and begins sucking on the left side of his neck. He tries to put his hands on her, but she only pushes them to the bed above his head.

She slowly slides her way down his chest, past his stomach, down to the towel. She looks up at him with a smile while biting the bottom of her lip as she undoes the towel, revealing his cock. All he can do is watch as she takes his semi-hard cock and begins licking around the tip of the head like a lollipop candy. The sensations force him to curl his toes. She puts it fully down her throat and he starts to moan.

Eventually, he pulls her off and pushes her over, onto the bed. Moving like a flash of lightning, he unbuttons and yanks her jeans and panties down. He grabs her by her thighs and pulls her toward the end of the bed. He stands and slams her legs open. He puts the head of his cock in and drives the rest of it deep into her. He puts her legs over his shoulders, grabbing onto her thighs.

He continues to thrust deep into her. She moans, "Fuck me...oh God, harder!"

He follows her request. "Oh shit JJ, I'm going to come," she says. He keeps thrusting harder, focusing all his energy on making her explode. He feels her start to tighten onto the shaft of his cock, but he keeps pumping harder.

She lets off a loud moan as her body starts to squirm from an explosive orgasm.

Knowing it's his turn, he begins slowing the pumps down, trying to hit the back of her pussy wall. On each pump, she takes her legs and wraps them around him, but he just keeps pumping away.

He starts to feel the edge of an orgasm.

She moans, "Oh yeah, baby." He can feel it coming from his toes into his cock. He pulls it out as it makes its way into the shaft. He grabs onto her as his body starts pulsating, allowing him to come all over her stomach. She moans, "Yeah, that's it,"

He has to catch his breath before speaking. "Where did that come from?"

"I don't know. I just saw you half naked and got horny as hell." She smiles as she kisses him. She pushes him off her. Now go get me a towel," she laughs. He hands her the towel he was using just minutes before. After wiping herself off, she gets up and gives him a huge kiss. "That's just what I needed before we go out," she says as she gets up to finish getting dressed.

About an hour later, they make their way to the club. The line is wrapped around the corner. He grabs onto her hand and pulls her behind him to the front of the line. As they reach the door, Jimmy is standing there.

"Hey, Jimmy. Have you seen Mark yet?"

"Yeah, he is in there somewhere. He's probably at the table I got you guys."

"Okay, cool. Thanks, Jimmy."

"Yeah, no problem."

The music is blaring as they make their way onto the first floor. The room is packed with people screaming and drinking. They walk toward the DJ booth.

"Hey, D-TEC. Have you seen Mark?"

"Yeah, man. He's running around here somewhere. He's all rolled out, Bro."

JJ just shakes his head. "Can you announce that I'm here, and tell him to come here?"

"Yeah Bro, no problem." The DJ gets on the mic. "Will my crazy ass homeboy, Mark, get your ass up to the DJ booth? JJ is in the house!"

JJ waves down a waitress and asks her to bring the bottles they ordered. They go sit on the couch and wait until the waitress comes back with the bottles. When she returns, he reaches into his pocket and pulls out $10 and hands it to her. She nods and walks away.

They begin drinking and dancing. After a few songs, he looks up to see Mark sitting at the table.

He takes Stacy's hand and leads her back to the table.

"Yo, Mark!" he shouts.

Mark takes a gulp before answering. "You made it!"

Mark laughs. "Yeah, man. You look fucked up, Mark."

"Yeah, I'm not going to lie, I'm fucked up."

"Did everything go okay tonight?"

"Yeah, I got almost all the money for you."

"Alright good, because I forgot my money at home, so you have to pay for the bottles," he says with a smile.

"That's fine. How much is it?"

"$200."

Mark pulls out four $50 bills from his left pocket. "Here you go."

JJ thanks him and puts the money in his pocket. A short time later, Amy shows up. "Stacy, look at you! Come on, let's go dance... Leave the boys to talk about their business."

Stacy gets up and walks off with Amy

He turns back to Mark. "That was smart thinking, talking about the concert tickets."

"Yeah, I figured you can call them that, and for the quality, you can call them by their rows.

Front row being the best, and nosebleed being the worst."

"Yeah, that's a good idea."

"So, you guys been having a good time?"

"Yeah, Bro. It's just a chill night for us, so just drinking. It looks like you're having a blast though!"

"Man," he says while shaking his head. "Them pills are great shit! Everything you get is good, Man. They are easy as hell to sell!"

"That's good to hear, but enough about that. Let's just enjoy the rest of the night. Grab your drink, and let's go to the dance floor with the girls." Mark picks up his glass, and the two of them head to the dance floor.

After enjoying a night of drinking and dancing, everyone regroups in the V.I.P section. Stacy looks tired and leans into him. "Honey, are you ready to go? I'm beat," she whispers.

He nods. "Yeah, I'm ready. Let me pay for this real quick." He flags down the waitress. "How much do I owe you?" he asks.

"Your bill is $200."

He reaches into his pocket and gives her the four $50 bills. Then he reaches into his other pocket and pulls out two $20 bills. "Here you go. This is your tip."

"Thank you very much!"

He nods and turns back to Stacy. "Okay Stacy, you ready?"

"Yeah, let's go home."

He turns and taps Mark on the arm. "Hey Mark, me and Stacy are going home. I'll see you tomorrow."

"Okay Bro, see you later."

The two girls hug, and they leave. He notices she can barely walk. "Hey, do you want a piggyback ride?"

She smiles. "You think you can carry me all the way home?"

He laughs. "I know I can, because I have to, so climb on." He picks her up and begins the walk home. What usually takes ten minutes takes him thirty. They both end up passing out as soon as they crawl into bed.

The next day, he wakes up to find a text from Leon waiting on his phone.

Hey I'm home. Come see me.

He gets up and gets into the shower. After getting dressed, he pulls out the shoebox in his closet with all the money and takes out two large bundles. He sticks them into his pockets and replaces the shoebox.

"Where you going?" Stacy asks from the bed.

"I got to run somewhere real quick. I'll be back in a few hours. Go back to sleep. I'll be back when you wake up."

"Don't leave. Stay here...stay with me. Do whatever you have to later."

He just shakes his head. "I'll be back before you wake up. Trust me, I'll be home."

"You better be," she replies.

"I will, I will," he says as he walks over and gives her a kiss on the forehead.

He gets into his car and heads toward Leon's house. While driving, he notices a cop following, behind him. As they pull up to the red light, he tries to relax.

*I don't have anything on me...*

The light turns green, and he starts to pull off. Not even a block or two past the light, the cop flips on the cherry lights. Nervous now, he pulls over. The officer gets out of his car and makes his way toward the driver's side. He rolls his window down. "Yes, Officer?"

"Do you know why I pulled you over?"

"No, Sir."

"You have a brake light out."

"Really, Sir? I didn't know that."

"Can I see your driver's license and registration please?"

He reaches in his glove box and pulls out the papers. "Here you go, Officer."

"You hold tight. I'll be right back." The officer returns a few minutes later. "Here you go, Son," the officer says, handing back his things.

"Thank you."

"Excuse me," the officer says. "Your vehicle smells like alcohol. Have you been drinking?"

"No, Sir."

"So, you wouldn't mind if I searched your car?"

"No, sir," JJ replies as he exits the car. He has nothing to hide.

The officer begins to search his car. First the driver's side, then the passenger side. As he reaches under the front passenger seat, he pulls out small baggie with five white pills.

"What's this?" the officer asks.

"What's what, Sir?"

The cop pulls up the bag and shows him. "What are these?" JJ just stares at the baggie.

*Shit... Mark rode in my passenger seat yesterday... He must have dropped them.*

"You're under arrest, Son."

"I'm under arrest?"

"Yes, now put your hands on the car." JJ turns and faces the car. A flood of emotions washes over him. The officer pats him down. "What do we have here?" the officer says as he starts to pull the money out of his pockets. "What is this? Drug money? Are you going to buy some right now?"

"No, I'm on my way to look at a car."

"Sure you are."

"Whatever Sir, believe me or not. I don't give a shit what you think. Put me in the cop car, so I can get bailed out and go home."

Now visibly angry, the cop forcefully puts him in handcuffs and pushes him into the back of his squad car. *That fucking Mark… What am I going to tell my parents?*

# SMURF

Smurf's right hook plants perfectly on the little nigga's chin. He can almost hear the nigga's jaw break as the guy tumbles to the floor. The dude on Smurf's left side lands a right hook to the side of his face, but he isn't even stunned. He still manages to land a three-punch combo to his assailant's face.

After landing that combo, he grabs the dude and slams him to the floor. The whole unit breaks into a massive roar. It's a total riot now, with everybody fighting, but that doesn't cause him to lose focus on his target. While he's beating on the little nigga, the other guy seizes the opportunity to catch him slipping. As the dude creeps behind him, carrying a sock filled with bars of soap, the guy is suddenly tackled to the ground from the side by Jeff, and he begins beating the shit out of him.

As soon as he rushes to help Jeff, the Orange Crush Team rushes in the yelling, "Everyone on the fucking ground, now!"

Instead of following a direct order, he rushes and kicks the little nigga square in the face and begins stomping on his head. The team shoots a laser dart that lands on the side of his body. Without a moment to think, the pain and convulsions from all the electricity running through his body drop him like a dead deer.

After securing the unit, and getting everyone back to their cells, the people of the Orange Team begin yelling, "Everyone take off your shirts and wait for an officer to come inspect your body!"

As the officers inspect the inmates, they pull anyone with fighting marks, bruised knuckles or blood on them to the hole. They grab up twenty-five inmates, including him, Jeff, OT, Drake and the two little niggas they were beating on.

After being escorted to the hole one by one, he is tossed into a cell. About twenty minutes later, Jeff is brought in and placed in the cell with him. More people get tossed into other rooms. OT gets put in a cell two rooms down from them. Drake, another friend, is placed five cells down on the other side of the hall. The two niggas are put in separate rooms on the top floor just above Drake.

"Who were them two little niggas, anyways?" Jeff asks.

"That's Teddy and Leo," he replies. "I've been beefing with them guys for the past few months. They tried to jump me a while back."

"Oh yeah?" Jeff's response is interrupted by people shouting through the chuck holes on the doors.

"Yo Jeff, where you at?" OT yells from his room.

"Yeah Family, I'm here. You good?" Jeff replies.

Drake yells from his room, "Yeah, we're good. You guys alright?"

A voice echoes from the top tier. "Where's that nigga, Smurf, at?" He hears them yelling, but doesn't reply.

"What's up, Smurf? Why you not going to reply to them niggas?" Jeff asks.

"Fuck them fools; I'm a real gangster. I am not in to all that wolfing."

"Shit, Family."

"Don't worry. I'm going to catch them little niggas out there on the block and smash their asses...and Smoke Junior's bitch ass, too."

The rest of the day is just a chill time to calm down from all the action that happened in the past few hours. The next few months feel like years as they sit in their six by twelve cell for twenty-three hours a day. They're allowed one hour of rec time each day.

After being in the hole for almost two months, the connection between Smurf and Courtney grows stronger through continued letters. While waiting impatiently one day for a letter from Courtney, he receives a letter from his lawyer, letting him know he will be visiting him next week to discuss events that could change the outcome of the case.

The next week feels like a lifetime as he anxiously waits for his lawyer to visit. On a midweek morning, he is awakened by the C.O., informing him of a legal visit.

After getting dressed and ready, he allows the C.O. to cuff him from the front and escort him to the room where his lawyer is waiting. As he enters the room, his lawyer stands and greets him.

"Hello, Mr. Davis. Can you take those cuffs off please, Officer?" The C.O. nods his head and undoes the cuffs.

"That's better," he lets out as he rubs his wrists.

"Go ahead and sit down, Mr. Davis."

He nods and sits. "So where have you been? I thought you died."

His lawyer folds his hands on the desk, visibly irritated at the comment. "If you must know, I've been going to bat, trying to find a flaw in this case. And then I find out that you've been in a fight. Now my question to you...is do you want to go home?"

"Fuck yeah, I do!"

"Then you need to stay out of the way, because I found a flaw in this case."

"What flaw?" he asks anxiously.

"Well, when the police did a photo array, they put your photo in with other individuals that you're associated with. They enlarged your photo to draw emphasis so the witness would point you out...and that is illegal."

"So what's that mean to me?" he asks.

"It means that you could be released and would never be charged with the crime again."

"Oh shit, are you for real?"

"I kid you not. I found a case where this happened, and the defendant was cleared of all charges. So it's just a matter of time before you're free. I put in a motion, and it's to be heard next week. You'll be getting another visit from me by the end of next week to let you know what's going on, okay?"

"Thank you, Roger. I appreciate all the work you're doing."

"Mr. Davis, it's my job. Don't thank me until you're free." They both stand and shake hands.

The C.O. comes in and handcuffs him to be escorted back to the hole.

Once back at his cell, he sees Jeff lying down and reading a book. Jeff turns and looks at him with anticipation. "So how did it go?"

He walks over to the table and sits down. "Well, my lawyer told me he found a flaw in some photo lineup."

"Oh yeah?"

"Yeah, Jeff. He said he put in a motion for a hearing next week, so I'll be seeing him again to find out what will happen next."

"That's great, Family! I Hope it straightens out for you."

"Yeah, me too, Jeff. Me too."


The next week goes by pretty slow. There's not much to do in a tiny room for twenty-three hours a day except sleep, shit and work out. As the date gets closer, he has trouble sleeping. His nights are spent wondering what happened in court.

It's now Friday afternoon,, and still no visit. He worries that something went wrong. The butterfly feeling consumes his stomach, making him sick.

*Straighten up. This shit is going to happen, whether you like it or not.*

Jeff and him are lying in their beds when a C.O. bangs on the door. "Davis, you got a visit."

He springs out of bed to get ready. They open the door, cuff him and take him to the room. As he enters, he sees Roger sitting. The C.O. un-cuffs him, then closes the door behind him.

"Mr. Davis," Roger says. "Sorry I'm late to see you. Go ahead and have a seat." He does as he is told and sits. "Well, you know we had a motion hearing this week."

"Yes, I know Roger. What happened?"

"Well they..." Roger says.

The butterflies in his stomach come flying back. Hesitation is never a good thing. He can feel the bile slowly work its way up his throat. "Well they what, Roger?"

"Well, you got a court date in thirty days from this last Tuesday, and they will be releasing you."

He sits back in his chair in a state of shock. He can't even think. Everything keeps running through his mind: the murders, his days in jail and now this.

"You okay, Mr. Davis?" Roger asks.

"Yeah...yeah, I'm good."

"Well Mr. Davis, I know this is a lot to take in right now, but do you have any questions for me?"

"Well I got one... You said they can't recharge me for this, right?"

"No sir, they cannot. When they messed up the photo lineup, they messed up the whole case, and they can't ever charge you with it again."

The thoughts running through his head are crazy. He just murdered three people and got away with it. He can feel the darkness fill his eyes as he thinks about the murders.

"So, I'm free?"

"Yes Sir, thirty days and you'll be free. So just kick back and relax and do us both a favor and stay out of trouble." He nods his head, as he stands up to shake Roger's hand, and thanks him for the great work he's done. "You're welcome, Mr. Davis. You have a second chance at life. Make this one count." He nods again and heads towards the door. The C.O. cuffs him and escorts him back to the hole. Back in the cell, Jeff's on his bed. His head shoots to the door as Smurf walks in. "I bet that was good news, wasn't it? You got a different swagger to you!"

He laughs. "Yeah, it was great news! Motion was granted. I'm going home!"

Jeff practically shoots off the bed. "No shit!"

"Yes sir, thirty days!"

"Fuck yeah, Family!" Jeff says as they do their handshake. "That's dope, Homie! Glad to hear it, family."

"Yeah, me too. I'm not going to tell Courtney though. I'm going to surprise her when I show up at her house."

"Yeah Man, that's good!"

"Trust me Jeff, I know!"


The next few weeks pass pretty fast as he and Jeff keep each other busy.

"Hey Smurf?" Jeff asks.

"Yeah?"

"What do you plan on doing when you get out? You hitting the streets?"

"Fuck yeah! I'm gonna go hard and try to make my million and get out."

"That's good, real good." Jeff replies.

"Why you ask?" he asks.

"Well, because kicking it with you, I can tell you are a real nigga. Not one of them fake-ass ones that mouths get a'flapping when the heat comes down. I want you to hook up with me and my partners.

We'll all make big money!"

"For sure, Jeff. I need a new gig and a spot if I'm really gonna make that money."

"Trust me, Family. These guys can get that million for you AND get you an unlimited supply. If you can unload it, they can supply it."

He grins and shakes Jeff's hand.

*Bet this will be a good business relationship.*

The next two weeks go by slow as hell. Waiting to get released is like waiting to go to Disneyland. The day finally comes, and he heads to the courtroom to meet his lawyer.

"Don't say anything; I'm going to do all the talking, alright?" his lawyer says. He nods.

As they sit down, the judge enters the courtroom and both parties rise. "You may be seated," the judge says. He proceeds. "We are here today for the case of Terrel Davis versus The State of Illinois. There is evidence that rules that illegal activities were committed by the government during a photo array, correct?"

"Yes, Your Honor."

"Both parties stand. Mr. Davis, you know you'll never be charged for this again, correct?"

"Yes, Your Honor."

"Well, on behalf of The State of Illinois, this case is dismissed. Mr. Davis, you're free to go." The judge pounds the gavel, finalizing the end of this ordeal. He knows that statement will play in his head forever. The day he beat three murder charges. This day will change him forever.

"Thank you again, Roger."

"Remember what I said, Mr. Davis?"

"Yes, I know."

Jeff is waiting again when he gets back to his cell. "So are you a free man?"

"Yes, Sir!"

Jeff laughs. "Alright, when you get out, go see Courtney. She will introduce you to my girl, and she's going to introduce you to my man, Papi. He will get you started and on your feet."

"Alright. Thanks, Jeff."

"No problem. Keep it real, Homie, and you'll be the nigga running shit out there one day!"

The next few hours go by slow, but they finally call his name. He says goodbye to Jeff one last time.

"Now don't forget, Smurf."

"Oh I won't, trust me." He makes his way through the release process and gets out to the fresh air. "Finally," he says as he takes a few deep breaths.

He has Courtney's address written down from the letters she sent. He goes to the nearest bus stop and waits for the number twelve bus. He gets off at the corner, just in front of a multicolored, ranch-style home. He stares at the house and then at the paper. "Here it is," he says. He starts to walk towards the front, his excitement building with every step.

*I'm going to pound this pussy.*

He gets to the door, knocks and takes two steps back. He begins to hear locks click from the other side. As the door creaks open, the silence is broken.

"No way!"

# JJ

The touch of the cold cement wall, and the chill from the old air conditioning system, keeps JJ alert and reminds him that this is not a dream. While he sits, rubbing his hand on his forehead, he imagines his parents' faces when he tells them the trouble he's in. He's not only disappointed in himself, but he's also angry at Mark.

*Why did he drop those pills?*

After about an hour of waiting, he decides to call everyone but his parents. Unfortunately, no one has a landline to answer his calls. The last remaining people he can call are his parents.

While he sits, staring at the phone and debating the call, he decides against it. With everything that has happened, he doesn't need a lecture or a screaming match. He waits nervously, not knowing what to expect. A C.O. approaches the door. "Jeremy, Jeremy Jepenski." He stands. "Come with me."

As the officer opens the door, he follows him down the hall to another room. "Take off all your clothing," the C.O says and points to the shower in the room. "Shower, then put these on." An orange jumpsuit, underwear and a pair of socks sit neatly folded on a metal table.

This is crazy to him. He was brought up by his family to follow the rules and to follow any orders given, so he does as he's asked. He showers, then changes into the jumpsuit.

"You ready?" the C.O. asks. He nods. "Okay, follow me."

He follows him into another room to get his fingerprints and pictures done. Now extremely upset, he stays completely quiet while going through the motions.

After the process is complete, he's escorted to a unit and given an ID badge to be worn at all times. They place him in a two-bed cell. Luckily for him, he has no roommate. He lies on the bottom bed and stares at the bed above.

*Damn it... I wish this wouldn't have ever happened. Fucking Mark...fucking Mark!*

After a short time, he finally starts to calm down and ends up falling asleep.

He wakes up to the C.O. telling him to get dressed. He has a court appearance. After getting dressed and leaving the unit, he sits down by the operation desk. Not knowing anything of the legal system, he turns to the female C.O. working at the desk. "They said I have court. What is that all about?... This is the first time I've ever been to jail."

She looks at him with no emotion. "Well, pretty much you go there, they tell you your crime and decide on a bond, so you can bail out of jail if you have the money."

"Oh, so you mean I can go home today, possibly?"

"Yes, you do have a good chance of getting out today." He nods his head as he takes a few deep breaths and then thanks her for her help. She nods, then goes back to facing her computer. Several minutes pass, then the female C.O. announces his name. "Jepenski, it's your turn."

He stands up and heads into the jailhouse courtroom. There are two men in suits, one standing at each table. The man at the left table waves him over. The guy looks young, probably only a few years out of college. He slowly makes his way over to the table. "How are you, Jeremy?"

"Well sir, I could be better."

"Just go ahead and relax. Let me take care of this." He nods in acceptance.

Everyone stands as the judge enters the room. "You can all be seated," the judge says. As everybody sits down in chairs, the judge looks to both tables. "Are both parties ready?"

The prosecutor and the public defender both reply, "Yes, Your Honor."

"Okay, let's get started. We are here for the case of Jeremy Jepenski versus the State of Iowa. This case involves possession of a controlled substance. Prosecutor, do you have any reason why this person should not be allowed bond?"

"No, Your Honor."

"Defense, do you have anything to say?"

"Yes, Your Honor. My client has never been in trouble before. He is a student at the local college here. I feel he should be released on a signature bond."

The judge nods. "Thank you, Counsel. Prosecutor, do you have any problems with that?"

"No, Your Honor."

The judge nods again. "Okay. Mr. Jepenski?"

"Yes sir."

"If we release you today, do you promise to show up to all your court dates?"

"Yes Sir, I do."

"Okay, we release you on a signature bond," the judge says, just moments before he slams his wooden mallet.

JJ turns to his lawyer. "Thank you."

His lawyer nods and gives him his card. "Come see me at this address tomorrow."

"Okay, I will," he responds.

He heads to the back of the courtroom and out to the waiting area. The female C.O. is still at the computer. He finds his same seat and sits. She looks up from the screen as he approaches. "So how'd it go?"

"Great! They're allowing me to go home on a signature bond."

"That's great. Congratulations."

"Thank you. I'm ready to get the hell out of here."

"I wouldn't blame you. Ready to go back to your unit?"

"Yes, I'm ready."

Once back at the unit, he waits patiently in his room for them to call his name. About forty-five minutes pass without any sign of a C.O.

*Man, maybe they forgot about me.*

Finally, he hears his name called and is told to pack his stuff. He grabs his belongings and throws them back into the plastic bag he was given when he first got there.

"I'm ready; I'm ready," he says in an antsy voice.

"Okay, go out those doors and meet up with the other C.O. They will take you to the release area so you can get your clothing and personal items back."

JJ nods and heads out the door. He follows the other C.O. down the hall to the release room, where he changes back into his street clothes before leaving. He has to sign some papers for his clothing before heading out the door. He steps out and takes a deep breath. He turns on his phone and calls Stacy.

"Hello," her sweet voice says on the other end.

"Stacy, can you come pick me up?"

He can hear the instant relief in her voice as she speaks. "What the hell, JJ! What the hell happened?"

"Just come pick me up. I'll tell you when you get here."

"When I get where?"

"The jail."

Her relief turns to shock and her voice goes up about five octaves.

"The jail! You were in jail?"

"Yes, I was in jail. Now, come pick me up."

"Fine, I'll be there in ten minutes."

He hangs up and looks back towards the building. Hopefully, this is the last time he'll ever have to see this place.

He looks up to see Stacy pull into the parking lot and stop. Seeing her familiar face puts him back in his safe zone, which eases the tension that had been building all night. Stacy gets out and gives him a huge hug and a kiss filled with more emotion and passion than he's ever felt from her before.

Tears of relief fill her eyes.

"I got pulled over for a brake light being out. The cop smelled alcohol from the night before, so he asked to search the car. I let him, not knowing that Mark had dropped a baggy of ecstasy pills underneath my passenger seat. The cop searched the car, found the pills and arrested me for possession of a narcotic."

"Well, at least you're okay, JJ. I've been so worried about you...I didn't know what to do. You told me you were gonna come home later. You never showed up, and you never called."

"Well, don't worry. I'm here now. Let's just go home."

Just the sight of his apartment door both comforts and angers him deeply. The thought of seeing Mark confuses him and makes him angry at the same time. They enter the apartment to see Amy and Mark sitting on the couch.

"Hey you guys," Amy says as she turns to see them walk in. He just nods and stays quiet.

"Hey Amy," Stacy says. "Come with me to the bathroom. I want your opinion on something. We'll leave the boys to talk."

He walks over and sits down in one of the chairs. Still, he says nothing. Mark looks at him with concern. "What the hell happened?"

"You tell me, Mark."

Mark's brows furrow. "What do you mean?"

"I got pulled over, and he found a baggie of ecstasy pills on the passenger side of the car. You know I don't ride on the passenger side of my car, so you tell me what happened."

"Are you saying it was me?"

"No, I know it was you."

Mark's tone takes on a hint of anger. "So what you want me to do about it?"

"There's nothing you can do, Mark. Your fuck-up jams me up. Just give me the fucking money you owe me. They took all my money that I had on me."

Mark reaches into his pocket and pulls out a wad of money. "Here's $1,000," he says and begins to count it out. "And here's the other $500, so the total is $1,500 that I owe you. I'm sorry, JJ...that you got in trouble. If there's anything I can do, just let me know. I'll help."

"Okay, well, for one, I need a ride to the impound lot to get my car."

"Alright. We'll take you." Mark calls out to the girls. "I'm taking JJ to go get his car. Do you guys want to stay here and hang out?"

"Yeah, that's fine," they reply from the bathroom.

When they arrive at the impound lot, they see cars everywhere: nice cars, junk cars and any vehicle you can imagine is there. They pull into the driveway and park. He goes to the front of the small, white metal building and walks up to the front desk.

"How can I help you?" the man behind the counter asks.

"Yes how can I help you?,"

"I'm here to pick up my car."

"What type of car is it?"

"It's a Honda Civic."

He searches the computer. "Oh, you're a lucky one. We just got it processed. Plus, it's the only

Civic we have on the lot right now, but before I can give you your car, I need your driver's license."

JJ nods and hands his driver's license to the man. The man does a couple double-takes from the license to the computer before handing it back. "Here you go. How do you want to pay for this?"

"How much is it?"

"It's $120."

He reaches into his pocket and pulls out the $1,500 in cash and counts out $120. "Here you go, sir."

The man prints out the receipt and hands it to him. "They will bring the car up to the front for you."

"Thank you," he responds, then heads back out to Mark's car.

"So, are they bringing your car?" Mark asks when JJ climbs back in.

"They're bringing it up front."

"How much did it cost?"

"$120."

"Damn, that's a lot of money for one day."

"Yeah, but what can you do? I need my car."

"Yeah, I guess you're right."

After getting his car, he heads back to his apartment to find Stacy lying down. He finally gets to fall asleep in his comfortable, large bed.

He wakes up the next morning from the alarm on his cell phone. He shuts it off and rolls onto his back. He needs to see his lawyer today.

*I don't want to go, but I huve to.*

After a ten-minute car ride, he pulls into the parking lot of his lawyer's office. He's already starting to get a little nervous. As he gets out of his car, he makes his way toward the glass, revolving door at the front of the tan brick building. He enters and makes his way to the front desk, where a beautiful brunette with black-framed glasses sits typing on a keyboard. He clears his throat and says hello.

"Oh, I'm sorry, Sir. I was so wrapped up in work, I didn't notice you. How can I help you?"

"I'm here to see my lawyer."

"What is his name, Sir?" He pulls out a business card. "Mr. Smith. Hold on one second. Let me page him." As she gets on the phone, he turns and looks out the window. A few minutes pass before he hears her again. "Excuse me, Sir?"

"Yes," he replies, turning around.

"He is the fourth door on your left, down that hallway," she replies as she points toward the hall next to the desk.

"Can I go down there now?"

"Yes, he's expecting you."

"Thank you," he replies, then heads down the hall. He counts the doors as he walks down the hall. When he gets to the fourth one, he knocks.

"Come in," a voice says from behind the door. As he enters the room, his lawyer stands to greet him. "Mr. Jepenski, have a seat."

"So, I came to see you like I was supposed to," he says.

"Yes, I appreciate you coming to see me so soon, Mr. Jepenski ..."

"Just call me JJ, please. Mr. Jepenski is my father," JJ interrupts.

"Okay, you can call me Mr. Smith or Derek, whichever you prefer. The reason why I wanted to meet with you is to get to know you and to discuss this case with you. Do you understand what you are being charged with right now?... The possession of a controlled substance."

"Yes, Sir."

"Do you know this charge could bring one year in jail and a fine?"

"No, I did not know this," he says, swallowing hard.

"Well don't get scared, JJ. I don't think that is going to happen. This is your first time getting in trouble, correct?"

"Yes."

"And you're attending college here?"

"Yes, I am."

"What is your major?"

"Chemical Engineering."

"Oh, really?"

"Yes, why? Is that bad?"

"No, but I actually used to attend college at ISU. You see?" He points to the diploma on the wall.

"I went there first before going to law school. I had a buddy that was in that field of study, I think...but I'm not sure. If you have a drug charge of any nature, you will be unable to find work in that field."

"Really? Are you sure?"

"I'm not completely sure, but I think this might be the end for you in that field."

Hearing those words crushes him. Everything he's ever wanted, ever known, is potentially gone because he took the rap for Mark.

For the rest of the meeting, everything the lawyer tells him goes in one ear and out the other. His body is numb from the complete and utter disappointment he has caused himself and his family, along with the thoughts of his dreams being ripped away.

"Hey, JJ."

"Huh?"

"You still with me, Buddy?"

"Yeah, yeah. I'm okay. Go ahead."

"Well, what I was saying is, with your lack of a criminal background, I should be able to get you probation. It will be on your record if they do not go for a deferred judgment."

"What is a deferred judgment?"

"It's a second chance. If you do good while on probation, it will come off your record."

"So, would I be able to get a job in my field of study, then?"

"I'm not sure, but I will find out for you though, okay? But do one thing... Don't worry about this. Just get back into school, keep busy and stay out of trouble. When I need you, I'll be in contact with you. I got all your information from the courts yesterday...okay?"

"Alright, Derek. Are we done yet?"

"I think we covered it all, JJ." Both men stand and shake hands. "Just remember, JJ...if you need anything, you have my card. Just call, alright?"

"I will. Thank you," he replies.

While walking out to his car, one thought keeps repeating in his mind.

*What am I going to do?*

# SMURF

"No way! Terrel? They let you go? What happened? Sorry, come in! Come in!" Courtney says while opening the door for him. She closes the door behind him and leads him to the living room. He finds a spot on a mocha-colored couch.

"Would you like something to drink?"

"Yeah, something cold."

"Okay, I'll be right back!"

He watches as her ass sways from side-to-side in her low, hug-to-the-hip sweatpants. He is already thinking about fucking her.

*God, I can taste it already.*

Upon her return, she hands him a cold glass of lemonade. "Here you go."

"Thanks," he replies and takes a few large gulps.

"So Terrel, what happened? Did they dismiss the case?"

"I found out they messed up the photo line-up, so they had to dismiss all the charges. I wanted to surprise you by showing up."

"Well, it definitely worked!" she replies as she hugs him. "Are you hungry? Do you want anything?"

"Do you have any steaks?"

"Hmm, let me go check." A few seconds later, she yells from the kitchen. "Yeah, I have one left!"

He gets up and makes his way to the kitchen to see her bent over looking into the fridge. He slides behind her quietly, grabs her by the waist and pulls her up against his crotch.

"Whoa," she says, giggling. "Calm down, Killa. You think you're going to get this that fast?"

"Probably not, but I was hoping so," he replies with a smile.

"We will just have to see," she says as she rubs her hand down his chest to the top of his pants.

"You want anything else with that steak? I got some collard greens."

"Yeah, I want those, too."

"Okay, go hangout in the living room and watch TV. I'll get this cooked for you. I'll yell at you when it's done."

He nods and heads back to the couch. After a while, Courtney's voice echoes from the kitchen. "Food's ready!" He throws the remote on the couch and heads towards the dining room area. At the small, wooden table, he finds a table set for one with his food and steak sauce bottles set out.

"Man, how I've missed food like this," he says under his breath. He turns to Courtney. "Smells great."

"I hope you like it."

He begins cutting up the steak. The meat is so tender and moist he almost doesn't need a knife. He takes the A-1 and pours it on an open spot on his plate. He takes a piece of the steak, dips it into the sauce and places it into his mouth. It tastes so good, he lets off a soft moan.

"That sounds like a good moan," Courtney says as she watches him eat.

"This food is great, Courtney. Where did you learn how to cook?"

"Just practice over the years."

He takes a second bite.

*Wow, this is better than the first...the sweet taste of freedom.*

He starts on the collard greens. Taking a bite, he gets flashbacks of his mom making them for him when he was little. After finishing his meal, he looks at Courtney. "You are an awesome cook."

"Well, thank you."

Once he's finished, she takes his plate into the kitchen.

"Need any help with anything?" he asks.

"No, go ahead and chill in the living room."

After she finishes cleaning in the kitchen, she comes and sits down on the couch next to him.

"So, did you have any plans for tonight?" he asks.

"No, but now that you're here, you want to have a chill night and just watch a movie?"

"Sure, sounds good."

"Okay, what do you want to watch?"

"It doesn't matter."

She nods and starts flipping through the channels. She stops when she sees the movie *Friday After Next*. The two of them relax on the couch as the movie plays. He puts his arm around her and draws her into him.

After a moment, she places her hand on his leg and slowly starts moving it up and down his thigh. He already knows what she wants. She smiles as he grabs her face and begins kissing her. As she puts her arms around his neck, he makes his way on top of her and starts kissing her neck, letting his hands explore her body.

He uses his hands to make his way up her back to pull her shirt over her head. Her fabulous C-cup breasts hang slightly. After tossing her shirt to the ground, Courtney grabs his shirt and pulls it off. He kisses from her neck down to her breasts, where he begins sucking and lightly biting her nipples, one at a time, until they are hard enough to cut glass. She moans as she rubs her fingers through his hair. He pushes her down on the couch and gets on top of her.

While testing the waters, he continues downward toward her belly button, kissing and caressing her body. He feels her start to push his head down. As he looks up, he sees her grab the couch with her other hand. He reaches up with both hands and grabs the sides of her sweatpants. He pulls them down to find that she's not wearing any panties.

He looks at her before pulling her pussy lips apart. Her sexy, bright-pink clit is semi-swollen. He starts licking it. Her loud moans and extreme wetness lets him know he's on the right track. Her shaking legs let him know of the coming orgasm. This doesn't faze him. He is focused on his mission. She finally orgasms, and he goes back on top of her and kisses her passionately.

"Hey, get up," she says. She follows him and then pushes him back down to the couch. She then sits on his lap, facing him, and begins to rub her breasts in his face, like a stripper. She slides down to her knees and unbuttons his pants. She pulls both his pants and boxers down and tosses them to the ground.

She grabs his cock with her right hand and his balls with her left. She starts licking the head lightly around the tip, then begins to suck and tug on the head with her lips. This makes him fully erect.

"Damn Terrel, you are super thick!" She smacks the tip against her lips and begins to lick the shaft, like a lollipop.

In a state of ecstasy, he's unable to talk. She starts twisting her hand along his shaft. As she puts it into her mouth, he grabs her hair and pushes her head down deeper on to his cock. She pulls it out and begins flicking the tip of her tongue on the v-part of the head. She begins to gently suck on his nuts. He can't handle it anymore. He picks her up and tosses her onto the couch.

She stops him. "Wait, wait, wait... Do you have a condom?"

"No, do I need one?"

"You're clean, right?" she asks.

"Yes, I'm clean."

"Fine, but I'm not getting pregnant," she says. She gets up and runs to the back bedroom. She returns with a brand new condom. He's still rock hard as he watches her put it in her mouth. She rolls it on to his cock, using her hand to guide it on.

"Fine, okay," she says. "Now fuck me doggie-style." As she gets up and bends over the couch, he slides behind and spreads her cheeks apart. He slides inside her.

"Go slow," she says as she starts to moan. He goes slow, until he is balls-deep inside her. He continues to do slow, deep thrusts into her super-tight pussy. Each thrust makes jiggles ripple through her ass. This excites him, and he pulls her hair back towards him, immediately hitting her G-spot and sending quivers throughout her entire body.

She begins to reach for his head, trying to get a grip on something. He pulls her closer and starts driving deeper into her wet pussy, feeling the tip of his head hitting against the back wall. He lets off a deep grunt as he wipes the sweat from his face. He reaches down and pulls both her ass cheeks apart and watches as his cock goes in and out of her.

He pulls out and flips her over. He spreads her legs and smacks the head of his hard cock against her swollen pink clit, then slides back up inside her. She lets off a loud moan as she arches her back.

With every deep, driving pump she moans. "Faster, faster…"

She starts to rub her index and middle finger on her swollen clit.

"Oh shit, Ma," he moans.

"What? What's wrong?" she asks, out of breath.

"The condom just broke and I'm about to bust. Where do you want me to come? Can I bust in your mouth?" he asks.

"Yeah, that's fine," she replies.

He pumps her about three or four more times, then pulls out. She hurries to her knees and begins to give him head while jacking him off. He can feel the orgasm coming, and the pulsating in his cock lets her know the orgasm's there. He lets off a deep moan as he releases a large amount of cum and frustration down Courtney's throat. She continues to suck on the head like a vacuum, trying to drain him of all the semen left in his body.

After finishing, she comes up and wipes off her mouth. "Now how was that?" she asks.

"That was the shit. That was some of the best head…and you've got the tightest pussy I've ever had. A nigga would kill for it!"

Courtney smiles. "I will be right back." She gets up and makes her way to the bathroom and then the kitchen. She returns with two glasses of soda and hands one to him.

"Thank you," he replies, then takes a few big gulps from the glass.

"I needed something to drink. You wore me out, Terrel. Plus, I need to wash that shit down, too," she says with a smile.

He begins to laugh. "Well, you know there's more where that came from."

She smiles and replies, "I know, but I'm sore and you wore me out!" She starts to laugh.

As the two sit cuddled on the couch he says, "When are you going to talk to Tanya again, because Jeff wanted me to meet up with her."

"I'm not sure when I'm going to talk to her again. Do you want me to call her?"

"Yeah, but not right now. This is our time. I got time for that after we finish what we started," he replies. The rest of the night passes, and they fall asleep in Courtney's bedroom.

The next morning, he wakes up to the smell of bacon and coffee. He stretches, rolls out of bed and makes his way towards the kitchen. The smells are overwhelming.

As he enters the kitchen, he finds her wearing nothing but an apron, making French toast and eggs. He sneaks up behind her and kisses her neck.

"Well hello," she says. "Good morning, Terrel."

"Good morning, Courtney. Did you sleep okay last night?"

"Great! Best sleep I've had in a long time," she replies. "What about you?"

"I slept great. I feel great today."

"Oh, before I forget to tell you...I talked with Tanya this morning, and she told me she is going to stop by around lunch time."

"Alright, cool. Thank you for calling her for me."

"You're welcome. It's not a big deal, Terrel. Go take a shower. By the time you're out, the food will be done, and we can eat breakfast."

He heads off to the shower while she stays behind in the kitchen. Once done and dressed, he heads back to the dining area to find a plate of food waiting for him. They enjoy a nice peaceful breakfast together.

"So, are you ready to go get some clothing?" she asks after they've finished.

"Yeah, that'd be great, actually." He follows her to her VW Jetta and climbs into the passenger seat.

"So where are we going?"

"I figured, since you just got out, we could run to the mall and get you some new fits."

"Really?"

"Yeah, no big deal. You need some new clothes."

After a few hours of shopping, they head back to Courtney's house with a few new outfits and a couple of pairs of sneakers to match.

As they eat lunch, a knock comes from the front door.

"Come in! It's open!" Courtney yells.

Tanya walks in, dressed in a pair of Apple Bottom jeans, a vintage T-shirt, and a pair of all white Jordans. "Hey girl," Tanya says.

"What's up, Honey? Come in," Courtney replies. He stands up and faces toward the door.

"And this must be Smurf," Tanya says as she makes her way in. "I've heard a lot about you."

"Well, hopefully good things."

"No worries. It's always been good."

"You want something to drink?" Courtney asks.

"Yeah, I'll take something cold if you have it."

"Yeah, I do. I'll be right back," she replies. She gets up and heads to the kitchen.

"So, Smurf, how was Jeff doing in there? Was he keeping you sane? He told me about the stuff you just beat. Congratulations."

"Thanks. It feels good to be free again. And yes, Jeff was keeping me sane. If it wasn't for him and Courtney, I would have probably blew up in there. Did Jeff tell you about me wanting to meet someone?"

"Yes he did, and I'll introduce you to him tomorrow when Courtney goes to work."

"Yes, that's probably the best. She doesn't need to be a part of this lifestyle."

Tanya points her finger at him. "Now let's make one thing clear, What you do outside of this house stays that way. Courtney is a great girl, and I do not want to see anything happen to her, you hear me?"

"I feel you. I am not trying to hurt her, either."

"I got the drinks," Courtney says as she returns. The two of them grab their glasses and take a drink. "So Tanya, what do you have going on today?"

"Nothing really, just hanging out. What about you guys? What are you up to today?"

"Not much. Just got back from the mall. I bought myself some new outfits and got Terrel some new fits and sneakers, too."

"That's cool. There might be something going on down at the pier tonight. You guys should come," Tanya says.

He looks over at Courtney. "Yeah, but it's totally up to Courtney."

Flo-Rida's song *Low* emanates from Tanya's purse. She grabs her phone and answers. "Hello. Hey, what's up girl? ... No, I'm at Courtney's place right now. ... Yeah, I can. When? 7:30 tonight? .... Yeah, I'll be there. Okay, I'll talk to you later."

"Who was that?" Courtney asks.

"Oh, one of the girls," Tanya says. "She needs a ride to the pier, so I gotta pick her up later. I got to go get ready, so I better get going. Smurf, it was nice meeting you. Courtney, Girl, you better come to the pier tonight."

Courtney walks her out and closes the door behind her. All he can do is watch Tanya's swagger as she makes her way out the door. If only he knew that she was the only ride-or-die type that would actually be able to keep up with him.

# JJ

Time passes by slowly as JJ waits to hear what's going on with his case. Days turn into weeks, then into months. He stays focused on school, tutoring and doing his research. He hopes that by staying busy, he'll forget about the trouble he has gotten into. The thought of what his lawyer told him that day keeps haunting his thoughts. Everything he has ever wanted in life...the successful job in the pharmaceutical business, the perfect life...all gone because of this drug conviction. He won't let the thought keep him from finishing school, gaining his degree and becoming successful in life.

He sits in his room, daydreaming in front of his laptop. All he can think about is his role model, Alexander Shulgin, and how he wanted to be just like him. The thought of the powerful Alexander knocks him out of his daydream and compels him to continue his research to create the ultimate chemical compound.

He searches and scans through websites containing information on drugs formulas, molecule displays and chemical effects on the human brain and body. Over time, he has built an understanding of drugs, why they are being abused and possible long-term effects on human beings. Each new site he visits is like a birthday gift. The information is new and undiscovered, and the feeling of excitement makes him giddy.

Not all sites are helpful, but that is the thrill and the feeling of accomplishment he gets from research. He has logged many hours, obtaining information on chemical drugs such as cocaine, ecstasy, heroin, LSD, THC and amphetamines. He now feels he has a good understanding of the drugs and their effects to a point where he might be able to synthetically duplicate and enhance them.

*Man, how am I going to get into the lab? Who could help me?*

He goes to his chemistry lab later that day to do some recruiting. While scanning the classroom, he sees George VanCleve, a scrawny, geeky-looking redhead with square glasses and freckles. George is the teacher's assistant.

*He is my best shot to get into the lab after hours. I know George doesn't have many friends, so maybe if I go over and small talk him, I can befriend him and get into the lab.*

He makes his way toward the table where George sits organizing his papers. "Hey, George."

George looks up in shock, pushes up his glasses and rubs his left hand across to his nose. "Um, hi JJ," he says in a shy voice.

"How are you, George?"

"I'm, uh, good. You?"

"I'm doing alright. Hey, I came over because I know you're really good at chemistry, and so am I. I'd like to meet and hang out with more people involved in the same stuff as me."

"Really?" George replies, visibly excited.

"Yeah, what are you doing tonight? Are you busy?"

"Nope, I'm free! Why do you ask?"

"Here's my number, George," he says as he writes his number down on a piece of paper and hands it to him. "If you want to stop by my house and chill tonight, just call my cell. Do you have a car?"

"No, I don't. I just ride the bus."

"Would you want to come over? I could pick you up."

"Alright, that sounds good!"

"Good! Well George, I gotta run. I'll talk you later."

"Okay, JJ. I'll see you later."

*This is going to be easy.*

When it gets to be about 8:00PM that night, his phone vibrates from an incoming call. The number is one he hasn't seen before. It must be George. His plan is playing perfectly.

"Hello," he answers.

"Um...yes, hi. Is this JJ?"

"Yes, it is."

"Hey, JJ. It's George."

"Oh hey, Bro. What's up?"

"Nothing, just calling to see what you are doing."

"I'm just hanging out at home. You want to come chill for a while?"

"Um...yeah...sure, alright."

"I'll come get you. Where do you live?"

"I live at the Larch dorms."

"Is this your number?"

"Yup."

"I'll call you when I get outside your building."

"Okay, sounds good."

"Pick you up in about thirty minutes."

He heads over to the dorms and calls George. George finally

appears in a pair of ankle-biter jeans and a plaid T-shirt.

*Wow, who dresses this kid?*

"JJ, thanks for picking me up," George says when he gets in.

"No problem. Let's go hang out at my place."

They get back, and he gives George a quick tour. His bedroom is their last stop. "This is my room. It's not very big, but it's a place to sleep."

"Hey, I like your posters!"

"Thanks. I've collected some over the years." George stares at a picture of Alexander Shulgin. "Do you know who that is?"

George looks at him, visibly insulted. "Are you serious? Any real chemist knows Alexander Shulgin. He's very well-known for his hallucinogenic chemicals."

"Yes, George. You are right. He is actually one of my favorite chemists...but come on, let's go chill in the living room. You want a soda?"

"Yeah, please."

"Okay, go ahead and grab a seat, and I'll get that for you." Moments later he returns with a soda and gives it to George. "So what made you get into chemistry, George?"

"I don't know. I've always had a love for science...ever since I was a little kid. What about you?"

"My mom works in the pharmaceutical business...plus chemistry is an adventure to me, so why not make it a living? Have you ever done anything on your own...like, try to make anything?"

George just laughs. "Well, I extracted all the caffeine out of four big boxes of those little tea packs and got three 100% pure caffeine pills."

"Oh yeah? Did you try them?"

"Well, that's the funny part. I took one, and it was too much for my body to handle. I started spazzing out and shaking really bad 'til it went through my body...then I was fine. What about you? Have you done anything like that?"

"Nope, just what I've done in class."

"Oh...well JJ, maybe sometime we can do something."

"Yeah, that sounds like that would be cool."

*Did this kid really just say what I think he said? This is going to be easier than I thought.*

Over the next few months, he and George become pretty good

friends. He even blows off Mark to kick it with George. He really wants to get on George's good side, so he can get into that lab.

He gets a call from his lawyer, telling him he will get probation if he pleads guilty and sets up a court date. The day arrives, and he is escorted into the courtroom by his lawyer.

"I see we have both parties ready to proceed," the judge says after entering the courtroom and sitting down.

"Yes, Your Honor," both parties reply.

"We are here for the case of Jeremy Jepenski versus the State of Iowa. Mr. Jepenski is being charged with the possession of a controlled substance. How would the defendant like to plead?"

"Guilty, Your Honor," he says in a nervous voice.

"Are you sure? Do you fully understand your rights to a trial, and the rights you will be giving up by pleading guilty?"

"Yes, Your Honor."

"Okay well, we, The Court, accept the guilty plea."

JJ looks at his lawyer. "And get a date soon. I want this to be done and over with."

His lawyer nods. "Excuse me, Your Honor."

"Yes, Council?"

"My client would like to rush the sentencing date."

"Prosecutor, do you have any problem with this?"

"No, Your Honor. We do not have any problems with this request."

"Thank you, Council. I'm going to set the sentencing for one month from today," he says, then slams his mallet.

His lawyer turns to him. "Now, don't worry about your sentencing. I talked to the prosecutor. They are asking for probation, so for the next month, just do what you regularly do. Don't worry about this. I got it covered, alright?"

"Okay," he replies, nodding his head.

Over the next few weeks, he spends his time split between Stacy, George, school and tutoring students to make money. Despite doing what his lawyer told him to do, that sentencing date still scares him.

*Fuck it. I want to party. I still got a few pills left. I'm going to call Stacy and George...see if I can get him to come out, too.*

He pulls out his cell and texts Stacy.

**Hey honey I want to go party. Are you free?**

the club? come pick me up!

**Hey is it okay if George comes too?**

That's fine. I don't mind.

**okay fine I'll be over to pick you up in a little bit, so be ready soon.**

He calls George. After a few rings, George answers. "Hello?"

"Hey, Bro. What's going on?"

"Nothing. What are you doing?"

"Nothing. Get dressed. I'm taking you out tonight."

George stutters slightly. "I don't know, JJ."

"Hey George, don't give me that. I am not taking no for an answer. You're coming, okay?"

There's hesitation on the other end. "Okay...where are we going?"

"I'm taking you to the club, so get dressed like you're going there, and I'll be over to pick you up in an hour."

"Alright, I'll see you then."

He leaves to get Stacy first. He pulls up in front of her apartment and honks. She comes out dressed in a pair of tight, Silver Tab blue jeans hung low on the hip and a white, V-neck T-shirt. As she opens the door, she smiles. "Hi, Honey."

"Hello, Sexy," he says, returning the smile. "I must admit, Stacy, you are looking fine as hell! I am going to have to keep my eye on you tonight."

She giggles and rubs her hand on his leg. "I'm all yours. No need to worry. This is going to be fun tonight, so let's do just that, okay? Do we have to pick up George?"

"Yeah, he lives at the Larch dorms. Will you text him and let him know we'll be there in five minutes, and to be waiting outside?"

Stacy grabs his phone and sends the text. She places the phone down on his lap and begins to rub his crotch through his pants.

He looks at her, smiles, and pushes her hand away. "I'm driving."

"So what?" she says as she unbuttons his pants. She unzips his zipper and pulls down his boxers.

He just smiles and shakes his head as she begins to lick him. She slowly puts him down her throat. He lets off a deep moan, but tries to focus on the road.

"Hey, you gotta stop. We are almost there."

"I'm not stopping until you come in my mouth," she mumbles. He now focuses all his energy to try to hurry. He starts to get nervous, because they're almost there, and he just can't seem to get off. She starts sucking on the head, which pushes him over the edge.

She lifts her head and laughs while wiping her mouth off. He zips up and buttons his pants as they pull up to see George standing outside waiting for them. He is dressed in a pair of khaki pants and a red polo shirt.

"Are you serious?" she says, laughing. "Is he really wearing that?"

"Don't laugh, Stacy. We'll get him better clothes at my house."

She just turns and shakes her head as she opens the door. George climbs in and practically falls into the back seat.

"Hey, JJ."

"Hey, George. This is my girlfriend, Stacy."

Stacy gets back in and turns around. "Hi, George. I think we've had a few classes together, right?"

"Yeah, it was math and English, freshman year."

"Yeah, you're right," she replies as she gives JJ a surprised look.

"Hey, we're going to go back to my place and chill before heading out, okay?"

"I'm still kind of nervous. I've never been to a club before.

"Trust me, bro... I'll make sure you have fun."

When the three get back to his apartment, JJ heads to his room, while Stacy and George sit in the living room.

"Hey, don't take this as any disrespect, but who taught you how to dress?" she asks.

"My mom...why?"

"Has she always dressed you?"

"Well, when I was younger. Now, I just like this style, so I dress like this."

"Well, today is your lucky day. I know a little about fashion, and you're about the same height as JJ. Can I do a makeover on you for tonight? Please, please, please?" she pleads.

"Um...I guess."

"Yes!" she says, jumping up in excitement. "I will be right back."

She goes into JJ's room and returns with a pair of Armani jeans and three button-down, long-sleeved dress shirts and three short-sleeve T-shirts. "Here, take these and go try them on. They might be a little big, but we got a belt to wear, too."

JJ returns to the living room, dressed and ready to leave. "Where's George?"

"He's in the bathroom. He let me do a makeover on him."

"Just don't mess with him too much, okay?"

"I won't, don't worry," she replies as she waves her hand at JJ.

He sits down and turns on the TV, waiting for George to return. George finally emerges from the bathroom, wearing a pair of faded blue jeans.

Stacy points her finger at him and curls her finger toward her. "Come here."

George looks like a scared puppy as he walks to her. She grabs JJ's shirts and pulls them up to see how each would fit. "How are your pants? How do they feel? Are they too tight? Too loose? They look like they fit okay. Turn around for me, George." George does as he's told. "Yes, they seem to fit pretty good," Stacy confirms. "Okay, George, take off your shirt."

She looks through the different shirts, deciding what color to put him in. She comes across a white long-sleeved button-down with skinny, lime green stripes. "Here, try this on." George puts it on, and it hangs on his lanky frame. "Hmm...going to have to put a T-shirt on you. We need something to draw attention to him, JJ."

"Hold on, I got something," JJ says as he heads to his bedroom. He returns with a bright yellow T-shirt with a picture of a smiling face, with a tongue sticking out, on the front. Above the face, black letters spell out *BON JOVI'S HAVE A NICE DAY.* "I got this at a concert a few years ago," JJ says. "It is too small for me, so I bet it'll fit you better."

George puts it on, and it fits perfectly. Stacy runs off to the bedroom and comes back with a white belt, accented with a silver, square buckle. "Put this on," she says, as she hands a shirt to George. After he puts it on, Stacy tells him to take it off again. She goes back to the bedroom and returns with a white long-sleeved shirt for under the T-shirt. "Here, put this on under the T-shirt," she instructs. George stays quiet and does what Stacy tells him. "What do you think, JJ?" she asks.

"Not bad, not bad. Fix his hair and tuck in the front of his shirt, so you can see the belt, and get some better shoes."

"Come on, George, into the bathroom," Stacy says, as she grabs him by the hand, and pulls him into the bathroom. "Now, take off your glasses. I want you to be surprised."

George's hair is about 2 inches long. She splashes water into it, then takes out styling gel and places it on his hair, massaging it into his scalp. She styles his hair into a faux hawk. "Don't peek yet," she warns. She tucks the front of the shirts into the front of his pants. "Okay, here. Put on your glasses."

George puts his glasses on, and his eyes grow wide. "You look great, George! I think JJ's got an extra pair of K-Swiss tennis shoes, too," Stacy says.

George, still in shock, walks out of the bathroom and into the living room. Still sitting on the couch, JJ looks over and does a double take. "Wow, Stacy! You did a good job! What do you think, George? You like it?"

"I'm, uh...still processing it all."

"All that stuff, what you got on, you can keep. It's all extra clothes to me, and that style suits you well."

"Here, George," Stacy says as she hands him the all-white tennis shoes. "Put them on."

"You can have those, too," JJ says. "They are just extras anyway...just a small gift from me to you."

"Thank you both. I really appreciate it!"

"No problem," they respond.

"Hold on, let me get a picture," Stacy says. She goes to her purse and pulls out a camera. JJ stands up and puts his arm around George's neck. "Say cheese," Stacy says with a smile, from behind the digital camera. The three of them look at the photo. Little do they know that this is going to be the start of a lifelong friendship.

# SMURF

"Are you almost ready?" Courtney yells from the living room.

He doesn't hear her over the sound of the shower. His thoughts are consumed by recent events. Anger builds as he thinks about Smoke Jr. and his partner, Yeo. He was fine, before they got him into all of this.

*BAM!*

The sound echoes in the bathroom after he hits the shower wall in frustration.

*Fuck it...them niggas gotta get it.*

The door swings open. "What the hell was that?" Courtney yells.

"My bad, Ma. I got lost in some thoughts, and I punched the wall. I apologize."

"You gonna be alright?" she asks.

"I'm good, I'm good."

*I have to be...*


They arrive at the pier just as the automatic lights kick on from the setting sun. They can hear the music blaring as they pull up. The place is filled with people laughing and drinking.

"Where the hell is Tanya?" Courtney asks, looking around.

"Shit, I don't know. Text her," he responds.

"I already did, and she hasn't responded yet. Let's just wait out here for a bit."

They walk to the side of the pier overlooking the water. Fading rays dance off the white caps.

"Can I ask you a question?" Courtney asks.

He doesn't take his eyes off the water. "What's up?"

"Well, this is kind of weird...but where do you see yourself in five years?"

"What do you mean?" he replies.

"Well, your goals in life... What do you want to do or be in five years?"

He finally turns away from the lake and looks at her. "Honestly, I'm doing me. I'm living day-to-day. I just watched my life almost get taken away for good. I'm just trying to have fun, enjoy life and make money. Why are you asking where I'll be in five years, anyway?"

"Smurf, I really like you, and I just don't want to get hurt. Plus, I'm not into that type of lifestyle that you were into before we met... I just don't know how I'd handle that."

"Courtney, I would never put you through that. That's something you don't need to worry about." He scans the area. "Man, where is this chick at?" he says in a restless voice.

"I don't know. Let me check my phone to see if she texted me back." She pulls out her phone. "I got a text. She's down at the restaurant toward the end of the pier."

"Alright, let's go. Text her and tell her to meet us outside."

Courtney nods. As they walk, he catches himself studying the people around him. He understands he's at war with Smoke Jr, and that he will take any chance to get him back. There's one thing that Smoke Jr. won't catch them doing, and that's slipping. Courtney, on the other hand, is focused on her phone.

They stroll through the large crowd of people until they finally are able to see Tanya waving at them.

"Hey, girl," Tanya gives Courtney a hug and nods her head at Smurf. "Hello, Smurf."

"What's up, Tanya?"

"Come on, let's go inside." Tanya grabs Courtney's hand and pulls her into the restaurant. He follows close behind. They reach a table filled with girls and their boyfriends. The sounds of Courtney's name being called echoes as each girl says her name and gives her a hug. The guys just look at him and nod. He looks around the table then sits down.

*These are some fake ass niggas.*

"We were just getting ready to order food," Tanya says.

"Good! I'm starving," Courtney replies.

They order their drinks and their food. Everyone is finished with their plates after an hour and a half.

"What is there to do?" one of the girls asks.

"Hey, let's go get on *The Spirit of Chicago*," Courtney replies.

"Yeah, that's cool," a few couples agree.

"Alright. Let's get this paid for and go get on the boat," Tanya says in an excited voice.

After the group leaves the restaurant, they make their way to loading dock. Once on the boat, the couples separate. A few drift to the bar, while others join scattered groups.

Tanya weaves her way to Courtney and Smurf. "What do you guys want?" she asks.

"Oh girl, you don't have to get us anything," Courtney replies

Tanya gives Courtney a crazy look and repeats herself with more force. "What do you want?"

"Okay, fine. I will take an Incredible Hulk. What about you, Babe?"

He looks at Tanya. "Get me a Henny and Coke."

"Alright, I'll be right back," Tanya replies. She is soon lost among the people.

Courtney goes over to the edge of the boat, and he follows behind her. "This is so pretty and relaxing, don't you think?" she says as she looks at the water below.

"Yeah, it's cool to come kick it and get away for a bit, that's for sure." He unconsciously turns his back to the water. He can't afford any surprises.

Courtney notices the subtle gesture. "Why did you just do that?"

"Do what?" he replies.

"Turn around so your back is facing the water."

"Ma, you have to understand... I'm used to being in jail. You always got to watch your back, because the day you don't is the day you get poked."

"Is it really like that in there?"

"Some of the craziest shit happens in jail. You just never know."

Tanya finally shows up with their drinks. "Here you go, guys."

"I think I need to use the restroom," Courtney says.

"You need me to come with?" Tanya asks.

"No, I'll be alright. I'll be right back," she says as she hands her glass to Smurf.

Tanya looks at him after Courtney's gone. "Are you having fun?"

"It's alright. Not really my scene."

"Yeah, Jeff didn't like this type of stuff, either."

He laughs. "I bet."

"What you mean?" Tanya asks

"Nothing. I just couldn't see him coming to a place like this, that's all."

"Well, he loves me and cares for me like you do with Courtney, so he would come just like you did."

"There ain't no doubt he loves you, Tanya. He always talked about you."

"Well, I'm not the only one he talked about. He always talked about you, Smurf. All the time." She takes a drink. "By the way, I talked to them people tonight, and I'm going to introduce you to them tomorrow."

"Okay."

"I'll meet you at Courtney's around 11:00AM tomorrow morning. Is that cool?"

"Yeah, but keep this hush-hush. I don't need Courtney knowing what I'm doing, 'ight?"

"Whatever you say, Playboy. I'm just doing what Jeff asked me to do. That's all."

"You're definitely a ride-o-die chick, huh?"

"Definitely not very many girls in the world like me, that's for sure," Tanya says with a smile.

"Enough about that."

"Sorry guys," Courtney says as she walks up.

"No big deal, Girl," Tanya says as Smurf hands the drink back to Courtney.

"Hey, do you girls want another one?" Smurf asks.

"Yeah, can I get another Incredible Hulk?"

"Sure. What about you, Tanya?"

"I'm okay, but thank you."

He nods and makes his way over to the bar. He returns with Courtney's drink after a few minutes.

"I'm going to leave you two love birds alone," Tanya says. "You two have a good time."

She walks off into the crowd, and they hit the dance floor. An hour or so passes, and Tanya returns to dance with Courtney. With a smile on his face, Smurf continues to dance with the girls. It's about 1:00AM in the morning when the boat starts to make its way back to the dock.

"Where you guys going to go after this?" Tanya asks.

"We have to run over to Terrel's mom's house so he can get his car. What about you?"

"I think I'm just going to go home. I'm tired," Tanya responds.

The girls hug one last time as they say their goodbyes. Tanya turns to him before leaving. "See you later."

They make their way toward Courtney's car. "Where are the keys, Courtney? It will be faster and easier if I just drive, then you can lead me to your house from there."

She nods and hands the keys to him. They arrive at his mom's ranch-style house about fifteen minutes later. He pulls into the driveway and parks.

"Do you want me to wait for you, or do you know the way?" she asks.

"I think I'm good. I need to grab some things anyway, so don't wait up. I'll be there after I get this stuff loaded. If you think you're gonna fall asleep before I get there, leave the front door unlocked."

"I'll see you soon," she replies as she climbs over into the driver's seat and gives him a kiss through the open door. She closes the door and slowly backs up and drives away.

He watches her pull away, then turns and makes his way toward the front. He bangs on the door. A few minutes pass as he hears a female voice yelling from inside. It's so faint he can't understand what's being said, but the voice gets louder as the woman gets closer to the door.

He hears the locks click and slide. "Why the fuck are you knocking on my door at 1:30 AM?" the woman yells. She falls silent when she sees who is standing in the doorway. "Oh my God, oh my God, Terrel, Honey, when did you get out?" his mom says. "Come on, come on and get your butt in here."

"Hi, Ma," he replies as he steps into the house.

"How long have you been out?" she asks.

"A few days."

"Are you doing okay?"

"Yeah, Ma. I'm good. I'm staying over at Courtney's. You remember...the girl that kept writing me."

"Oh yeah!"

"I just stopped by to grab some clothes and my Tahoe. Go back to bed. It's late, and you have to work in the morning. I'll be back in a few days to visit you, okay?"

"Alright...I love you, son. Please be safe."

"I love you too, Ma. Now get to bed." He helps her into bed and shuts the door behind him.

He makes his way down the stairs to his room. He goes to his bed and flips up the top corner of the mattress. His bed frame is old oak. It's small, but very sturdy. A few years ago, he was able to rig a compartment in the frame under the mattress.

He pulls out about an ounce of work and $5,000 in cash, plus a half-ounce of Purple Haze hydroponic weed. He fills his pockets with the hidden items and finds a gym bag to load with clothing.

Once packed, he pops open the back hatch of the Tahoe to reveal three fifteen-inch subs. He tosses the bag to the side and pulls out his keys. He sticks a key in a small hole on the side of one of the speakers, and the top of the center sub pops out. He pulls it, lays it down and pulls out a small, all-black 9mm handgun and another $2,000 in large bills. He then places the gun and money back into the speaker box, then begins pulling out everything from his pockets and placing it in the box.

Once everything is in the box, he replaces the speaker and closes the hatch. He starts up the SUV. The snarl of the V8 engine rumbles in the early morning. He sits back in the seat and takes a deep breath.

*Man, I've missed this.*

He backs out of the driveway and makes his way toward Courtney's. She's already sleeping. He tosses the bag onto the ground and crawls into bed with her.

The next morning, he wakes to Courtney's lips on his. "I'm going to work, but I left my spare key on the kitchen table so you can lock up when you leave," she says. "I'll be back later. Tanya called this morning and said she'll be here around 10:00AM, so be up and ready." Courtney gives him one more kiss and leaves.

After getting dressed, he runs out to his car and grabs the weed out of the hatch. He gets some cereal, then sits down on the couch and starts to roll a blunt. After finishing his breakfast, he lights up.

"Come in! It's open!" he yells when he hears a knocking on the front door. Tanya walks in.

"Yo Smurf, what's up? Damn, I smell it!" She laughs. "Let me inhale it!"

He waves her over to the couch and passes the blunt to her. As she takes a couple hits from the blunt, he puts on his shoes and gets ready.

"Hey, Smurf. Before we go see this guy, we need to stop and see Jeff first. Is that cool?"

"Sure, that's cool...but let's take my truck, alright?"

At Cook County Jail, they go through the pat-down and metal detector searches and are led upstairs to the visitor's area. Tanya sits down and he stands close behind her.

Jeff sits down and smiles. "Hey, Ma."

"Hi, Honey," she replies.

"What are you guys doing?"

She smiles. "Nothing too much. Figured it would be nice to come see you."

"Thanks for coming to see me. What's good?"

"Oh, nothing. Just kicking it with Smurf."

"I see that," Jeff says as he nods to Smurf.

"Everything okay in there, Honey?"

"Yeah, I'm good. I'm going to need some more cash soon. Maybe within the next few days."

"How much?"

"I don't know, like $200 or $300?"

"Okay, I'll get that on your books in the next day or two."

"Okay, I love you."

"I love you, too." She gets up and Smurf sits down.

"How's the free life?" Jeff asks.

"It's straight. I've just been kicking it. What about you? Life alright in there?"

"Yeah, Fam. Same shit, different day. You know how it is."

"Well Jeff, keep your head up, Family. You'll be home soon."

"Hey, have you met the dude yet?"

"Not yet. That's next."

"Okay. Just be yourself. I already talked to the dude through her, so you're good."

"Alright. Thanks again, Fam, for helping me out."

"No problem. Just don't forget about me, you feel me?"

"I feel you, and I won't."

"Oh Smurf, before I forget...remember them little ass niggas we got into it with? Junior's boys?"

"Yeah, them fools... What about them?"

"They just got released, so keep your eyes and ears open, you feel me?"

"Good looking, Fam. Thanks for the heads up."

"Our visit is almost up. Thanks for coming to see me. And remember...be yourself when you meet the dude."

"Alright, for sure. Keep pressing, Homie."

"Yeah, you too, Smurf."

Jeff gets up and heads back to the unit. They go out to the SUV and head toward downtown. They pull into a parking ramp and drive around to find a place to park. Once parked, they walk down the street to the Rainforest Cafe. The hostess greets them and asks how many are in their party.

"Actually we're meeting someone here," Tanya says.

"Okay, go take a look," the hostess says. Smurf follows behind as Tanya scopes out the place, looking for Jeff's friend and partner. In the back corner, away from everyone, sits a short, mixed-race man with wavy black hair.

"There he is. Come on," Tanya says, leading him over to the table.

When they walk up, the man looks up, and then stands. "Tanya, hello," he says.

"Papi, this is Smurf," she replies.

Papi looks at him. "This is the famous Smurf I've been hearing so much about." The two shake, hands and they all sit down. "So, how long have you known Jeff?"

"I've known him for years, but just hadn't really bumped heads."

"Heard you were just in jail for...what? A triple homicide?"

"Yeah."

"How did you beat it?"

"Damn Fam, you got a wire on or something?" Everyone begins to laugh. "So what's good? I hear you're the man to talk to about what I want."

"Well, this isn't the place, nor time to talk about it. I'll give you my number, and you can call me later."

He nods. "Yeah, true story. We can work it out from there."

Papi turns to Tanya. "How's Jeff doing?"

"He's good. We just came from seeing him. He asked for money, so I'm going to be sending him $300 later."

Papi reaches into his pocket and pulls out four $100 bills.

"Here, give this to him, and tell him it's from me."

"Thanks, Papi," she replies.

"Shall we eat?" Papi asks. They decline. "Well, I guess this is it then," Papi says and reaches over to shake Smurf's hand. "Here is my number. Hit me up later. Tanya, it's always a pleasure."

"See you later, Papi," she replies as she shakes his hand.

Smurf notices some awkward movements from the person sitting three tables down. "Hey, Papi, tell your goons to be more discreet. I noticed them when I first came in, and as I shook your hand, they were staring hard. When I shook it again, they were staring hard again."

Papi faces him. "You're good kid, very observant. Either that, or they're dumb," he says and laughs.

After the meeting, they leave the restaurant and make their way back to the truck.

"I didn't even notice those guys," Tanya says outside the

restaurant.

"Shit Tanya, I watch everything. I notice everybody. But what are we going to do now?"

"Well, let's head back to Courtney's. I need to get my car. I got some running around to do. Gotta drop that money off to Jeff."

Once back at Courtney's, Tanya gives him a hug and tells him she'll see him later. He waits until she is gone to get into the hatch again. Seeing that no one is out, he pops open the speaker hatch and pulls out his 9mm pistol, places it in the waist of his pants then climbs back into the driver's seat. He places the gun underneath the seat and heads toward the gas station.

*I can stop there, get some gas, wash my car and grab a cigar.*

As he enters the parking lot, he spots the top half of Yeo popping out of a white Cadillac. He pulls up behind it to block the car in. He watches Yeo walk inside. The darkness fills his eyes as he thinks back on the chain of events leading up to today.

He reaches under his seat and grabs his gun. Yeo walks out of the gas station and up to his truck. He sees Smurf's SUV, but he can't see who is sitting in the driver's seat through the black tinted windows. Yeo walks back to the driver's side and taps on the door. "Hey Family…

you're blocking me in."

# JJ

"Are you ready?"

JJ looks up to his lawyer, standing in a black, three-piece suit. "Yeah Derek, I'm ready to get this over with." He follows his lawyer into the courtroom and proceeds to the defendant's table. He observes the rest of the courtroom, trying to understand the court system and how everything works.

*I have to know what I'm dealing with if I'm going to keep selling.*

One of the guards in the courtroom yells for everyone to rise. The residing official is Judge William Spitzner. The judge enters and sits down. "You all may have a seat," the judge says in a deep voice. "We are here today for the case of Jeremy Jepenski versus The State of Iowa in a criminal case for the possession of a controlled substance. Today is the sentencing date. Are both parties ready to continue?"

"Yes, Your Honor," the prosecutor and Derek say.

"After standing alright in this case, the plea agreement states that if the defendant pleads guilty to one count misdemeanor possession, the state recommends a deferred judgment and one year of informal probation."

"That is correct," the prosecutor says.

"Does the defense have any objections with this plea agreement?"

"No, Your Honor," Derek replies.

"Mr. Jepenski, you have full understanding of the crime you are about to be sentenced for today? And, you weren't promised anything the plea agreement doesn't contain? You also understand you're giving up your right to forego trial?"

"Yes, Your Honor. I do understand, and no promises were offered outside of my plea," he says in a calm voice.

"Alright, thank you, Mr. Jepenski. Do you have any questions or concerns before I go ahead and sentence you?"

"Yes, sir. I would like to apologize for my actions. This won't happen again."

*I just won't get caught again.*

"Thank you, son," the judge says. "Will the defendant please stand?" He rises from his seat. "I hereby sentence you to one year of informal probation. You will be ordered to complete at least four urinary analysis tests over the period of the probation. You are to report to the probation office within forty-eight hours. Court adjourned."

JJ looks at Derek and extends his hand. "Thank you."

"No problem, Jeremy" Derek responds as he accepts his hand. "I'm just doing my job. Now, stay out of trouble and get this behind you."

"Trust me, I'm going to stay out of the way, that's for sure."

"Good. Good luck to you, Jeremy."

JJ grabs his paperwork and leaves the courtroom. Once outside, he turns on his cell phone. As he walks to the car, his phone starts vibrating from missed calls and voicemails. He calls his voicemail. "You have two messages. First message... 'Hey honey, just wanted to tell you good luck. Call me after you're done in court. I'll talk you later.'"

He deletes the message.

"Next message... 'JJ, it's George. You must have your phone off. Call me back when you can.'" He deletes the message and calls George.

"Hello," George says when he answers.

"Hey, George. What are up to?"

"Nothing, really. What about you?"

"Nothing, really. You told me to call you. What's up?"

"I remembered you asked about getting into the lab. Well, are you free tonight around...let's say 6:00PM?"

"Seriously? Are you for real? You aren't just messing with me, are you?"

George laughs. "No, I'm being for real."

"Okay, sounds good. I'll see you there."

"Okay, George. I will see you later." After hanging up with George,

he calls Stacy.

"Hey JJ," she answers. "So did you get probation?"

"Yeah, they gave me one year probation."

"Where are you at?"

"I'm on the way home. Why?"

"Oh, I just wanted to see if you wanted to come hang out for a little

bit."

"I'm sorry, Honey, I can't. I'm super busy. How about tomorrow?"

"Okay, that's fine. We'll hang out tomorrow."

"Okay. I'll call you later."

"Talk to you later."

By this time, he's already made it back to his apartment. He tosses

his keys onto the kitchen island, grabs a soda and heads to his bedroom.

He gathers all of the miscellaneous notes and documents from his

research and tosses them into his backpack.

Just before 6:00PM, he makes his way to Truman Hall, the science building on campus. Not knowing where to meet George, he sits on the stairs outside the building entrance.

After waiting for almost twenty minutes, he picks up his phone to call George. Almost simultaneously, he hears his name being called from a distance. He looks around, but sees no one looking at him and doesn't see anyone he recognizes. He hears his name called again, louder this time. He looks around again and sees a skinny guy running and waving his arms in the air. As the guy gets closer, he notices its George.

*What the hell is this kid doing running, looking all crazy?*

George is out of breath when he finally reaches him. "So sorry. Sorry I'm late."

"It's cool, man. Why were you running?"

"I was running late in a study group, so I ran here from the library."

"Hey Bro, you could've just called instead of running."

George laughs. "No, no...I forgot my phone at home."

"Oh...well take a breather, catch your breath."

"No, I'm good. I'm good. Let's go in."

JJ shakes his head. "If you say so. Let's go."

They walk into the old, four-story, brick building. The place was built in the early 1900s, but it's kept its character. While walking down the hall, George turns toward him. "So, what do you need to do in the lab anyways?"

"Oh, just doing some research."

"Oh, I see. Do you need any help?"

"I might. I will let you know."

George pulls out a set of keys when they get to the door, looks around, then hurries to unlock it. "Hurry. Come in, come in," George says. George closes and locks the door behind him. JJ looks around the all-white room. It's filled with stations equipped with glassware of every shape and size.

"George, do you have access to chemicals?"

"I got access to some. Why?"

"I need some stuff to test."

"Okay...to test what?"

"This," he says, pulling a baggie of commercial-grade marijuana and a baggie with ten ecstasy pills from his pocket.

"What are you trying to test with that stuff?"

"I'm just curious to find what major chemicals are in these and also how to extract them. That's all."

"You're doing extractions?"

"Well, yeah. Do you know about them?"

"Of course! Have you done them before?" George asks. He shakes his head. "We're going to need some stuff over there." George heads into another room and returns with some chemicals. "We're going to need these to do the extractions. Oh, and I can't forget the heat lamp."

"Heat lamp? What do you need a heat lamp for, George?"

"I will explain it to you. Just give me one sec." George leaves him at one of the stations and comes back with a heat lamp. He lays everything on the table in a row.

He points to a big silver can. "This is anhydrous acetone...and that heat lamp is for those pills.

Alcohol works better for stuff like this, but it usually takes longer. Since there is little to no water in this chemical, there is no moisture...which means it evaporates extremely fast. Now JJ, I need you to do me a favor."

"What's that?"

"Can you take that weed and clean it and crush those pills while I prep the lab? Then I'll show you how to do the extraction."

"Okay, no problem." He makes his way to the end of the table and begins cleaning the weed and crushing the pills into fine powder. He watches as George sets up the lab, trying to memorize every move. He notifies George once he's finished.

"That's a good job. Now come on." George nods toward his station. "Basically, the concept is very simple with the ecstasy, which is also known as MDMA in our world."

"How do you know about drugs?" JJ asks.

Georges smiles. "There's a lot of stuff you don't know about me...but yes, I know my fair share about synthetic drugs."

*Maybe you CAN be more useful after all.*

"Back to what I was saying. The concept is very simple," George continues. "MDMA is not soluble in the acetone, so what it will do is remove the cuts and binders and leave you with pure MDMA."

"How did you learn all this?"

"I might look like a geek. I might act like a geek. I might dress like a geek...but secretly, it's just a front. I've known about stuff like this for years. I've been into science since I was a little kid. As times go by, you try different things and experiment. So, probably like you, I did research on things and messed with them. Now I'm teaching you what I had to teach myself."

"George, this is crazy. You just don't seem like that type, but I guess it's those types that know it all. I appreciate you helping me with this."

"Hey, no big deal. I owed you a favor for helping me out with those clothes. But anyway, pass me that powder, will you?" He nods and hands it to him. George gets a flute and dumps the powder into it. "Now, what you do is you take the acetone and pour it onto the powder and shake. What will happen is the pure MDMA will sit at the bottom. After we let it sit, we grab this filter and place it over the glass, then pour the contents onto the filter. After we do that, we allow it to drip free of liquid, then move the filter to another jar and run more acetone through it."

"What is this doing?" JJ asks.

"What it's doing is making sure all the impurities are removed from the final product."

"Oh really? Now I understand what you mean!"

After running the product through three or four washes, they finally let it drip until it stops, and place the powder on a glass plate.

"Now, we turn on the heat lamp to help speed up the process of drying out this powder. Once it's dry, it will be very crystallized," George explains. "That's when we know it's done. Let's go ahead and leave it in here until 8:00PM. We'll check back on it. Now JJ, we are going to do the same thing with the marijuana, but I want you to try to do it yourself. I'll help you if you need it, but the only way to learn is to do."

He begins to follow the instructions, one step at a time, remembering what George did and duplicating his movements. He washes it a few times and places it over the heat lamp. Now, it's a waiting game.

After a few moments of silence, he turns to George. "George, can you take a look at something for me?"

"Yeah, sure. What is it?"

"A formula." He pulls out a paper from his bag and hands it to George, who instantly starts looking over it like a kid in a candy store. Several minutes go by, and George says nothing. He's so focused on what he's reading that he barely blinks. After he finishes, he hands it back to JJ. "This formula was definitely written by a novice."

"What do you mean?"

"I understand the steps, but these chemicals will slow down the process. There are other chemicals you can use to speed up that process. The hard part would be to crystallize it at the end. You would need methane gas to do so, but it's definitely doable."

*Damn...this kid's good.*

George looks at him and gives a little smirk. "You don't want to try to make this, do you?"

"Do you think we can?"

George hushes him. "I don't know. I don't want to get into any more trouble than I could have already gotten into."

"You won't, George. Who's gonna tell? Only me and you."

"Will you give me some time to think about it? That might be a little too much to chew right now."

"I appreciate your honesty, and if you could...if you decide not to help me, can you please act like this conversation never happened and don't discuss what I'm doing with anyone?"

George nods as they stand by the heat lamp, admiring their work. George looks at him. "Do you have anything to put this in?"

"Let me look in my bag and see if I got some type of plastic wrap... Would that be okay?"

George shrugs. "That's fine."

He searches through his bag and finds a wrapper to put the powder in. "Here, let's put it in here."

"Alright," George replies as he begins scraping the final product off, into the wrapper. "What you need to do is take that back to your house and spread it on a mirror evenly and let it dry overnight. Hopefully, by then, it'll be completely dry and ready for consumption. We didn't get much out of this, which proves my theory that what you had was not good."

"And what about the drying of the THC?"

"Well, it is the same concept as what we did with the other, but what we need to do is pour it into a cup of some sort, so we can get back to the house. And, we need to clean this place up. It needs to look like no one did anything." JJ nods in agreement and helps George clean up the lab.

*I'm still in awe that George knows as much about this stuff as I do.*

Once the lab looked the same as when they arrived, JJ asks, "George, question, Do you ever think someone could create a super drug?"

"Hmm...what do you mean?"

"Well, a more powerful, yet safer, drug than what's on the streets today... Like a drug that you could take and still pass a drug test...or maybe even control it and only let it work when you want it to."

George hesitates before speaking. "I'm not sure what to tell you. I mean, I think anything's possible... It just depends on people and how willing they are to get what they want."

He looks at George with a newfound respect and nods his head. He offers to give George a ride home, and they walk together to JJ's car.

He pulls up to the dorms, and George gets out. "Thanks again for the ride. I appreciate it!"

"Yup! You have a good one."

"Thanks. You, too!" George shuts his door, and he watches him sprint up the stairs of the building.

*I wonder if I pay him some cash off this stuff if he will help me.*

When he gets back to his apartment, he grabs a black bowl out of the cabinet and heads into his bedroom. He sets the bowl on his desk, pulls down the medium-sized mirror from his wall and places it next to the bowl. He pulls out the powder and the marijuana liquid from his bag. He spreads the powder on the mirror and pours the liquid into the bowl.

"I really hope this works," he says. "I guess we'll just have to wait and see."

After getting it all organized, he lays on his bed and texts Stacy. While waiting for a reply, numbers fill his head. All he can think about is how much money he can make in a year...or even five.

His phone vibrates from a text

Hey honey. I'm chilling at home studying. What are you doing?

**I just got home from running around and I'm chilling now. Do you want to come over tonight?**

He presses Send and returns to the numbers.

*I wish I could make money like some guys do in the movies. Man, I'd give my left nut to have that kind of money!*

Another text interrupts his thoughts.

I can't. I have class early in the morning. Don't you have to go to see your probation guy tomorrow?

*Oh, shit...she's right. All this messing around today, I forgot about that!*

He thanks her for the reminder, and they say their goodnights. Before crawling into bed, he stares one last time at his experiment. "Man, I hope this works." His thoughts drift to his meeting tomorrow.

*I hope they don't fuck with me, or this is going to be a long year...*

His thoughts are crowded with numbers again. He closes his eyes and smiles.

*I'm going to be rich. Filthy rich.*

# SMURF

The darkness fills Smurf's eyes as he stares at Yeo. He rolls down his window. Yeo's eyes brighten as recognition sets in. "Yo, Smurf! When did you get out?"

"Not too long ago," he replies as he slowly puts the gun back under the seat.

"I heard you got caught up on a murder case, Smurf."

"You can say that...yep," he responds.

*I just wanna blast this nigga.*

"Well, Family, I'm glad to see you back out. I got something to help you out, but you'll have to meet me on the block around 1:00AM tonight, 'ight?"

"Yep, I'll meet you there," he replies.

*This nigga...he is up to no good. I think he's up to something, but I'm going to catch his ass slipping.*

He throws his truck into drive and pulls off.

*I'm going to go down there at midnight... If he's planning anything, he'll be trying to do it early before I get there...*

-----

Midnight arrives. He leaves Courtney's house to make his way down to the spot. He parks two blocks away, so Yeo won't know he's already there. Dressed all in black from head to toe, he gets out and pulls his burner from under the system's speaker and puts it in his waist lining. He makes his way toward the spot, using the shadows for cover.

*I can't let him see me.*

Once he's within safe viewing distance, he waits.

*I'm going to catch this little nigga slipping.*

He spots Yeo's Cadillac. He makes his way over, sliding in as close to the car as possible. He can hear Yeo talking on the phone. "Yeah man, he'll be here at 1:00AM…. Yes, he doesn't suspect a thing. He thinks I'm giving him something." Yeo goes silent for a while.

*He thinks he's gonna catch me slipping. This nigga got something coming!*

He focuses his attention again as Yeo continues. "When do I get my money?"

Smurf feels his anger swelling.

*This nigga sold my ass out!*

"Just be here at 1:00AM, alright? He'll be here. And bring my money!" Yeo yells, then hangs up.

Smurf looks at the time on his cell phone.

*Man, it's only 12:30AM. I still got thirty minutes...I'm going to wait and blast this fool around 12:50AM. And I really do hope that was Smoke Jr. on the phone, because if it was, I'm going to kill his bitch ass, too.*

He watches as Yeo works the block.

*Man, this little nigga isn't doing too bad, actually. Too bad it's his last night.*

He puts his phone on silent and readies himself. He takes a few deep breaths before pulling out his 9mm burner from his waist and clicking off the safety.

As Yeo exchanges drugs and money with some man, he slides out from the midst of the shadows and slowly approaches from the rear. He aims his weapon at the Yeo's back and fires one shot, hitting him in the neck.

As he watches Yeo tumble to the ground, he turns the gun on the dazed man and lays a round into his head. After watching the man fall to his knees, he turns back to Yeo. He's still alive, but bleeding badly. He stands over Yeo and looks down at him. Yeo stares back at him, unable to speak.

Smurf shakes his head and begins yelling. "Punk-ass nigga! You killed yourself, Family! Shouldn't try to make deals with the wanna-be devil! I know you sold me out, Yeo!" In his blind anger, he aims the burner at Yeo's face and fires one last shot.

While fleeing the scene, he notices a black Ranger Rover with a set of 24' rims creeping up the

street.

*That has to be that nigga, Smoke Jr.*

He hides behind a parked car, waiting for the SUV to get closer. As it pulls up, he sees some familiar faces. Smoke Jr. is in the passenger seat.

*There he is.*

He crouches, making his way toward the slowing vehicle. He hops up and aims his gun at the side of the SUV and starts to open fire.

*BANG! BANG! BANG!*

The sound echoes from the gun as the shells tumble to the ground. He unloads six shots into the backside of the SUV. He runs off, not pausing to see if he hit or missed.

He hits a dark, poor'ly lit alley and breaks out into a sprint. Bullets are already whizzing past him. His car is still a few blocks away. As he approaches the location of his SUV, he slows his pace. He walks slowly so he doesn't draw attention to himself. He gets in and starts driving back to Courtney's.

*I need to get rid of all of this...the clothes, the gun, everything.*

Back at her house, he places the 9mm back in his secret spot in the speaker and walks in to lay down with Courtney, who is sleeping peacefully.

Soft hands on his stomach wake him the next morning. "Good morning, Terrel. Long night last night?"

"Hey Ma," he replies as he leans in and kisses her on the lips, allowing him to avoid her question.

"You hungry?" he asks.

"Yeah, I'm starving," she replies.

"Alright, well let's go make some breakfast." They both get up and go into the kitchen and make breakfast. Courtney does most of the work; he just messes with her.

They both sit down on the couch and turn the TV to WGN. The news at ten comes on. The reporter is a young, dark-haired tan-skinned woman in her early thirties. "Thank you for tuning into WGN news at ten. Our next story is a case of a drug deal gone bad."

He keeps eating his food, but focuses on the newscast. He needs to keep his emotions in check. The reporter continues. "A fatal shooting left two men dead and two other men wounded last night on Rodger street in the north side. Two individuals have been arrested for having possible involvement in the case." Two young, black males are pictured on the screen. The photos are of Smoke Jr. and some guy named Blake Smith. "Both men are being held without bail in Cook County Jail. Both men have a history of felony convictions and were also in possession of firearms. We will keep you updated as more information is released." He laughs.

*Damn, those niggas are hit! Bye bye, Smoke Jr.!*

"Hey Terrel, didn't you grow up in that area? Do you recognize either of those guys?" she asks.

He looks up from his plate. "Yeah, I grew up in that neighborhood, but I don't know them." He pauses. "Hey, don't you have to work today, Courtney?"

"Yeah, I do here in a little bit. What are you going to do today? Are you going to go job searching?"

"Yeah probably...see if I can't find something," he says.

*I really got to go burn all the evidence and get rid of that burner...*

He goes back to his food, but she doesn't take her eyes from him. "Terrel, I'm proud of you...that you're trying to better yourself. A lot of people won't do that...but I better go get ready. I need to be to work here in an a few hours. Good luck with the job search," she says, then leans in and kisses him.

After she's done getting ready, they kiss again, and she leaves. He sits down on the couch and exhales.

*I'll give it about an hour, and I'll burn that stuff.*

After about forty-five minutes of waiting, he heads to the bedroom and grabs his clothes. He brings them into the kitchen and goes to retrieve his shoes. He steps out onto the patio and places all of the items on the ground. He starts up the grill and waits for it to heat up.

Once the grill is ready, he tosses the clothing onto the grill and sprays lighter fluid into the grill. He can feel the heat as the flames engulf the clothing. He lets the clothes burn for a half hour, and then he tosses the shoes and jacket onto the grill, spraying more lighter fluid.

*Now we wait.*

For the next hour, he waits inside. When he goes back out to check on the progress, he is hit with the smell of burning rubber. Thick, black smoke rolls from the grill in angry waves. After most of the smoke clears, he sees only ashes of what used to be evidence to his murderous endeavors.

*How am I going to dump this ash out? I can't just leave it here in the yard.*

He goes inside and finds a large plastic container. He takes it out to the grill and scoops the ashes into it. When he's finished, he places the container on the counter and goes into the laundry room and grabs the bleach from the cupboard. He brings the bleach into the bathroom and gets undressed and starts slopping it all over his body--anywhere that could have gotten gunpowder residue. He does his upper body first, then his lower, making sure not to let any spot go untouched. He finishes by taking a hot shower.

After he's done, he heads back to the living room and sits down on the couch. He picks up his cell phone.

*Alright, it's time to call.*

He grabs his phone from his pocket and scrolls until he reaches Papi's number. A few seconds go by as he waits for Papi to answer.

"Hello," the deep voice says on the other end.

"Hey Papi, it's Smurf. You good?" he asks.

"Yes, come see me when you're available."

-----

The next eight months are a blur. Smurf's come up is so fast that he doesn't have time to think, let alone blink. Smoke Jr. is in jail, Yeo is dead and he has no more problems. Only thing now is getting the product out fast enough to feed all the hungry mouths.

With his street wits, and Papi's unbelievably great product, he feels untouchable. If anyone in the south half of Chicago is getting cocaine, they arc buying it from him. He has a double life, This life and the life Courtney knows. She doesn't know that the business he works for is actually just a front, set up by Papi to keep him clean and wash the money.

As the money starts rolling in, he starts running out of spots to keep it. He has hiding spots everywhere. He even buys a safe for Courtney's, just to have some extra play-money in case they need it. His life is so fast-paced that he doesn't have time to catch his breath.

*Thank God Jeff will be home soon. I need a right-hand man to help... This is becoming overwhelming.*

-----

His phone vibrates. Tanya's name shines bright on his screen.

"Hello! What up, Homie?" The familiar, friendly voice is Jeff's.

"Jeff, you out?"

"Yes sir, Family! Where you at?"

"I'm at Courtney's."

"Alright, I'll be over in a bit. We are on our way."

"Alright Jeff, I'll see you soon."

A knock echoes through the living room a short time later. "It's open! Come in!"

Jeff and Tanya enter. "What's up, Fam? Long time no see!" Jeff says, a huge smile stretching across his face.

"Glad to see you home, Jeff." They do their handshake and then a quick hug. "Feels good, doesn't it?"

"Fuck yeah, Fam! That shit was getting out of control. I was going insane in there!"

"Well, your ass is home now. I've been waiting for a while now."

"Yep, finally home. So Smurf, I was hearing your name running around... Papi really hooked you up!"

"Family, if it wasn't for your help, I would have never made it to where I am right now." He pauses. "I'll be right back, Jeff. I got something for your ass." He heads to the back room, where the combination safe is, and pulls out ten large stacks of $100 bills.

Back in the living room, he sits down and places the money on the table. "Here you go, Jeff.

Welcome home."

"Ah damn, Family!" Jeff replies in a happy, yet confused and excited voice. He almost doesn't know how to react.

"You're my right hand man, Jeff. None of this would have been possible if it wasn't for you, so this is your take. I've been saving it for you. Also here," he says. He tosses Jeff the keys to his Tahoe.

"You need a car, right? Well you just got one."

"For real, Family?" Jeff replies.

"Yep, for real...and it has a dope stashspot. I'll show you."

"True story!" Jeff says as he places the keys next to the money on the table.

"Yeah man, I told you before...if I fuck with you, which I do...that if I get rich, you get rich. All I had in jail was my word, and you stayed loyal to me, so now it's my turn to show you some love and show you how I get down.

"Yeah, I feel you." Jeff replies. "How much money did you just give me?"

"I dunno, Family...like...roughly a hundred grand, give or take. I just split it two ways...plus investments into other things that are yours as well, but that's for another time."

"Seriously, Smurf? A hundred grand?"

"Thats what I said, isn't it? Do with it what you want. It's your welcome home gift. Enjoy it."

"I really do appreciate it a lot."

"Not a problem, Family. It's good."

Jeff turns to Tanya. "You know about this, Tanya?"

She just smiles. "Yeah...I kind of already knew about the money. We just wanted to surprise you."

Jeff turns back to him. "How can I ever repay you?"

"You can't, Jeff. I won't allow it. Just stay loyal to me, and we'll both be so rich we won't know how to spend all the money."

Jeff nods, and they shake hands on it. "Let's get rich together."

-----

Months pass as the two partners hit the streets. Business is cracking. They are running competition in the hood dry. Their business is booming so much that they can't get the product fast enough.

"Hey Terrel, I have a question to ask you," Courtney says one night while they're watching TV.

"What's up?" he responds.

"We've been together for almost a year now, and I was curious...if I was to get a job in New York City, would you move with me?"

He hesitates before answering. "Are you serious?"

"Yes, I'm serious," she says in a somewhat pushy voice.

"Damn Ma, relax. Why do you wanna know anyways?"

"Well Terrel," she says in a snotty voice, "I got offered a job in New York City, and I wanted to see if you'd move there with me...and that will tell me if this thing we got going is for real or not."

He thinks of everything going on. Everything he's worked so hard to build, but he also wonders about the possible opportunities this could bring. Possibly even the expansion of operations to New York City.

*I guess New York couldn't be too bad, right?*

# JJ

The anticipation fills JJ's stomach as he stands in front of the old, brick building. A sign in front displays the large letters: DEPARTMENT OF CORRECTIONS PROBATION OFFICE.

*Man, I hope this guy ain't a dick.*

"Excuse me," he says after he reaches the desk.

A short woman with brown hair looks up from her work. "Yes?"

"Yes, I'm here to see my probation officer."

"What is your name?" she asks.

"Jeremy Jepenski."

"Okay, go ahead and have a seat, and he'll be with you soon."

Ten minutes pass as he waits nervously. "Jeremy Jepenski," a manly voice says from behind.

He turns around and stands up. "I'm Jeremy."

"Follow me," the man says. He is a short, pudgy guy with dark hair. They walk down a narrow hallway. JJ looks around, observing area locations and people, trying to overhear conversations in rooms as they walk by.

"In here," the man says, opening the door to his office. "Have a seat." He walks into the man's office and sits down. He scans the room and notices many certificates and awards hanging on the man's wall.

The man sits down across from him on the other side of the desk. "So, you're Jeremy."

"Yes, Sir."

"Well, my name is Brian, and I'm going to be your probation officer for the next year of your informal probation. You were convicted of drug charges, is that correct?" JJ nods. "And you do know that the judge has ordered you to complete at least four urine drug tests, correct?"

"Yes, Sir. I know that."

"Do you work, Jeremy?"

"No, I'm a full-time student."

"Are you in college?"

"Yes, I go to ISU."

Brian smiles. "Oh, that's my alma mater."

"Oh, really? You went ISU?"

"Yes, I did, but enough about me, Jeremy. I want to set some ground rules. For one, I'm a straight shooter. Don't lie to me, and I won't lie to you."

*This dude seems pretty cool.*

"Can you follow those rules, Jeremy?"

"Yes Sir."

"That's good. Now, I see here that you have a probation fee."

"Which is how much?" he asks.

"It's for $400."

"How am I supposed to pay for it?"

"Do you want to set up a payment plan?"

"No, I'll pay it all out when I come to our next meeting."

"Alright. I have all your information. Do you want to set up a meeting for next month, now? If you have any problems making it to the meeting, you need to call me to reschedule. That's one thing I expect from people that I have on my caseload: Responsibility." Brian begins to look through his schedule for next month. "Okay Jeremy, I got you down for one month from today. Any time that day is fine, just make sure that you make it here that day."

"Okay," he says, nodding. "Are we all done here then?"

"Yep, you're good to go. I'll see you here next month," Brian responds.

JJ gets up and leaves, making his way down the hallway towards the front door. After reaching the parking lot, he takes a long, deep breath before getting into his car.

Back at his apartment, he heads to his room to see the final results of their experiment. He first stares at the MDMA powder. As he looks at it, he remembers George saying it will look like salt. He studies and checks the powder. It looks like fine grain salt. Out of the baggie of pills he had, it looks like half came back in the form of this powder. He puts it back and checks out the bowl where the liquid THC was.

*This must be the powdered THC. Now what did George say again about adding the powder to high-grade alcohol to make liquid THC? I wonder what alcohol I can use... I wonder if Everclear will work.*

He reaches into his pocket and pulls out his phone to text George.

Hey George can I use Everclear for that experiment?

While waiting for a response, he pulls out the digital scale from his closet and weighs the MDMA powder. It comes out to be 700 milligrams.

*Most pills are 150 milligrams, so I guess you could say that I got four-and-a-half pills out of the ten pills I had... That's not bad. And I can* *sell them for more...at least $25 each...maybe even more.*

The beeping from his cell phone interrupts his thoughts. He flips it open.

hey JJ that Everclear is perfect. use about an eighth of it and mix it and walla. you need an eyedropper so go find one or buy one. They're decent priced, but hey I gotta go. hit you up later.

JJ closes his phone.

*Damn, I need to get Everclear and a dropper. I better run to the store.*

After returning from the store, he takes the supplies to his room. He carries the eyedropper and an eighth of Everclear to the table, then opens it and starts scraping all the THC powder in the bowl into a pile. After all the powder is together, he pours it into the Everclear bottle.

Once all the THC powder is in the bottle, he puts the lid back on it and begins to shake it slowly. After shaking, he places that off to the side and grabs a couple plastic baggies out of the shoebox in his closet, along with the skill shovel, so he can scoop the MDMA powder into baggies. After weighing the MDMA powder to 700 milligrams, he begins scooping and bagging the powder in 150 milligram increments. He puts the powder in each corner of the baggie, then tears it and ties it up.

*That's one. Only three-and-a-half more to go.*

He continues to bag up the rest of the MDMA powder. After the powder is bagged, he scrapes together the rest on the scale, licks his finger and rubs it across the scale, picking up the extras on his fingertip and places it in on his tongue. The instant bitterness makes him cringe.

*This is some good shit!*

He hears the sound of the apartment door opening and closing. Mark is home. "Come in here real quick, Mark! I got something for you!" he yells through the door.

Mark steps in. "What's going on?"

"I got some molly."

"Molly? What's molly?"

"It's pure MDMA powder. Molly stands for molecule."

"Really, JJ? You got pure MDMA powder?" He nods and hands over a baggie of the MDMA powder. "So I see that you got it all bagged up."

"Yeah, Mark. Sell them for $25 each or all of them for $100."

"Is it really good?"

"Yeah, I just tried some. Bitter as hell, Bro."

"You just tried some?" Mark asks. "I thought you were on paper."

"I am, but I don't have to see my P.O. 'til next month. The stuff is in your system maybe, what, three days, tops?"

Mark reaches in to his pocket and pulls out two $50 bills and hands them to him. "Here, I'll take them all."

He hands Mark five small baggies. "Let me know what you think of them. I have one more thing!" He picks up the bottle of Everclear and fills the dropper with the liquid. "Open your mouth," he says.

"What?"

"Trust me, Mark. Just do it." Mark opens his mouth and sticks out his tongue. He squirts a few drops out for Mark. "Give it about ten minutes and come back and see me."

Mark nods and leaves the room. Twenty minutes later, Mark is back. "What is that stuff?"

He laughs. "It's our work."

"Whatever it is, I am high as fuck right now!"

"What type of high?" he asks.

"Shit...a mind and body high! So what is it, JJ?"

"It's liquid THC."

"Liquid THC?" Mark asks.

"Yes, so instead of having to smoke it, you just put a few drops on your tongue and keep it moving."

"Are you trying to sell it, JJ?"

"Yeah, probably. Maybe for $1 a hit. Why?"

"Well JJ, I don't want a hit. I want the whole bottle...so, how much will a bottle run me, Bro?"

"I don't know...how about...let's say $400 for the bottle."

"Well, I only have $200 on me. Can I get you the rest of the money later?"

"Yeah, that's cool. Go ahead and take it." Mark grabs the bottle and dropper and heads off to his room. He returns to give him the first half of the money and disappears back into his room.

JJ lays on his bed and looks at the ceiling, dreaming about a life of riches. The life everyone wants, yet only few seem to reach. He grabs his cell phone to text George again.


hey you got time to stop by? if so let me know.

He closes his phone and falls asleep. After about an hour, he notices his phone flashing. He rubs his eyes and slowly picks up his phone.

hey JJ I can stop by here in a few hours. I'm on campus tonight so I'll call to make sure you're still home.

He closes the phone and lays back down for another forty-five minutes. Ringing from his phone wakes him up. Stacy is calling him. "Hello?"

"Hi, Honey," she replies.

"What's up, Stacy?"

"Oh nothing, just calling to see what you're up to."

"Nothing really, just lying down. You want to come over?"

"Sure, if you want me to come over."

"Okay yeah, come on over. The door will be open."

"Okay, see you soon," she replies.

"Okay, see when you get here."

After hanging up with Stacy, he hears Mark yell through the door.

"Hey man, you awake?"

"Yeah!" he yells back.

Mark opens the door and steps into his room. "Hey, I got that other $200 for you." Mark hands him ten, crisp $20 bills.

"Damn, Mark! You sell it that fast?"

"Yeah, I sold a quarter of it for $200, so we're even now."

"Yep, we're straight."

"Hey, JJ?"

"Yeah? What's up?"

"Hey, when are you going to be getting that molly?"

"Probably tonight."

"Okay...well if you do, let me know what's good, okay?"

"Will do," he replies as Mark leaves the room. His phone rings again. This time it's George.

"Hello George," he answers.

"Hey, JJ. Are you at home?"

"Yeah, I'm here. Are you going to stop by?"

"Yeah, in about twenty minutes. Is that cool?"

"Yeah, I'll be chilling with Stacy. Plus, I got something for you."

"What is it?" George asks.

"You will see when you get here."

"Okay, I'll be there soon."

He hears the front door open after a while. He gets up and makes his way to the living room to see Stacy standing in the hallway with a red tank top and short red shorts. "Well hello," he says.

She smiles and starts to laugh. "Oh shut up, JJ! I've missed you."

"I missed you too," he replies as they give each other a hug and a kiss.

They make their way to the couch and sit down. "So what's going on tonight?" she asks.

"Nothing, really. Just relaxing, watching TV. You want to watch something?" he asks as he passes the remote to her. She shrugs and grabs the remote. "Are you thirsty?" he asks.

"Yes, can you give me an ice water?"

He gets up to get a couple drinks, when there is a knock at the door. He opens the door to find George standing there in a plain, white T-shirt and plaid shorts. "What's up, JJ?"

"Not much, come in."

"Okay. Stacy, what are you up to?" George asks.

"Hey, George. Nothing much, just hanging out."

"Hey, George, close that door," he tells George. George closes and locks the door and makes his way over to the empty chair in the living room. JJ makes his way back to his seat and hands Stacy her drink. "Hey Hun, find something good to watch? Me and George have to talk real quick in the back."

"Okay, but make it quick," she says.

"Come on, George, follow me." He leads George back to his bedroom and closes the door behind them.

"What's up, JJ?"

"I got something for you."

"What is it?"

He pulls out a wad of money and counts out $400. "This is yours."

"What? Mine? For what?"

"That's your cut of our science experiment from last night."

"What do you mean 'my cut'?"

"I sold all of the stuff we made. You did half the work, so this is your cut." He places the money in George's hand.

*Even though I really gave it all to him, this will attract him more to help me.*

"Really, JJ? It's that easy?"

"It's that easy, George. Less than twenty-four hours and you already made $400. Not bad for little-to-no work, huh?"

"Now I know why people do it if it's that easy! Why isn't everyone doing it?" George asks.

"Not everyone is made to do it, do you know what I mean?" he replies.

"Yeah, I know what you mean."

"It's not something for the weak. So have you thought about my offer?" he asks.

"Yes, and after tonight, I'm very interested...now that I can see how easy it is...but let me see if there is an easier way for us to do it."

"Go ahead, George. Take as much time as you need...but you're in for sure?"

"Yeah, I'm in!"

They shake hands. "Not a word to anyone, you hear me?" he says.

George nods. "Yes, not a word to anyone."

"Enough about that. Let's go back out with Stacy before she starts asking questions. You want something to drink?"

"Yeah, you have soda?"

"Yeah, we have cans, is that okay?"

"Yeah, that's fine."

"Okay, go sit down, and I'll get it for you." They leave his room, and George makes his way over to a chair, while JJ grabs a couple more sodas from the fridge. Stacy breaks the silence. "So are you boys done talking now?"

"Yeah, we're done. Just some guy stuff," George replies.

*Man, the kid is pretty good on his feet.*

He tosses a soda to George and sits next to Stacy. "Find anything good?"

"*Fast and the Furious*...is that okay, Honey?"

"Yeah, that's fine. What about you, George... Is that okay?"

"Yeah, that's fine."

She starts the movie and snuggles into him. He puts his arm around her, but looks to George.

"Hey, George, are you into cars?"

George shrugs. "Not really, are you?"

"Yeah, I like imports and exotic sports cars. Hopefully, one day I will get to own one or two."

"That would be nice, but a little expensive, don't you think?" George asks.

"Yeah, but what's the point of dreaming if you're not going to dream big?"

"Well JJ, I guess you're right. I usually just look at things for being real and obtainable."

"Anything is obtainable, George. You, as a person, limit yourself from obtaining what you want in life. You only live once, so enjoy it."

"Hush!" Stacy says. "The movie's coming on."

*I wonder where I will be when I'm fifty.*

He leans down and kisses Stacy on the head.

*It doesn't matter where I'll be in the future. All I know is I'm happy now.*

After the movie, George stretches and stands. "Well guys, I'd love to stay, but I think I'm going to go home and crash. I have a long day ahead of me tomorrow."

"Do you need a ride? We can take you home," Stacy says.

"No, no, don't worry about me. I'll be fine, Stacy. It's always a pleasure."

"Yeah, you too, George."

"JJ, hit me up tomorrow, alright?"

"Okay, Bro. Will do," he says.

"Okay, guys, I'm out of here. Have a good night."

"You too, George," Stacy replies.

He gets up and locks the door behind George. "You want to lay down, Stacy?"

"Yeah, let's go to your room."

They go to his room and snuggle under the blankets. "Hey JJ, can I ask you a question?" Stacy asks.

"Yes, what's going on?"

"What did you and George need to talk about?"

"Some stuff that...is better that you don't know. And don't need to know. It's just better that you don't know everything, Stacy."

"I guess," she replies in a pouty voice.

He leans over and kisses her on the lips. "Don't get upset, alright? There are some things you don't need to be involved in...and this is one of them, okay?"

"I'm not mad; I just like to be involved in stuff."

"I know you do, that's why I said just not this one."

His phone rings. "Who is that?" she asks.

"It's Mark."

"What does he want?"

He's too busy reading to answer her.


Hey bro this party is way better than with those white strippers!

the people I'm with want to know when the next party is.


He begins to smile. "What is it? What does it say?" she asks.

"He's just fucked up somewhere, sending me goofy texts."

"Oh," she responds.

He closes the phone and tosses it on the ground, then rolls over

and wraps his arm around Stacy.

*I just struck gold.*

# SMURF

After a long moment of dead silence, he grabs her hand. "Courtney, I love you very much, but I just don't think I'm ready to leave the city." Tears slowly start to form in her eyes. "Don't cry, Ma. You know what?...how about I'll help you buy a nice house in New York and help you sell this one so you can get extra money? I promise to visit you one weekend a month...and when I'm ready, I'll move out there...deal?"

"You promise, Terrel?"

"I promise." They kiss. "Let's celebrate you getting a good job in New York, tonight," he says.

"What you want to do?"

"I don't know...call Tanya, and we can go out on the town tonight," he replies.

"Okay, I'll call her," she replies as she picks up her cell and walks off towards the back room. He kicks back on the couch. All he can think about is the business. It's moving so fast, and the profits are so great. He can't leave the city.

She returns from the bedroom. "I talked to her, and she said her and Jeff will be ready to go by 10:00PM tonight, and they will meet us here."

Tanya and Jeff get to the house a little after 10:00PM. "What's up? What we on?" Jeff asks.

"Well, Courtney just got a new job in New York, so I figured we could go out for dinner and a movie."

"Hey, Family, let me holler at you for a minute," Jeff says.

"Alright, Jeff, let's go on the patio." Once on the patio, he closes the sliding glass door behind them. "What's going on, Jeff?"

"Well, this little nigga named Quick needs a half book and a nine piece."

"Alright, Jeff, so what's the problem?" he asks.

"Well, I only got a nine... I was hoping you would have eighteen, and I could get it from you and get you back tomorrow."

"Well, Jeff, all I have is eighteen left...but if you need it, I got you. Plus, I re-up tomorrow."

"Alright, thanks, family."

"No problem, Jeff. When is this supposed to be done?"

"Anytime I can get it, he will take it."

"Okay, well tell him you'll have it for him tomorrow morning, because we are going to go have a good time with our girls tonight," he replies. "Now, come on, enough about business. Let's go out and enjoy ourselves."

Back in the house, they make their way to the living room to find the girls chatting away.

Courtney looks up. "Are you boys ready to go?"

"Yeah, let's get going."

-----

After a long, fun-filled night of dinner, drinks and an action-packed movie, they all head back to Courtney's house. Once back, the girls head to the back bedroom while Jeff sits with him in the kitchen.

"Hey, do you think I can get that eighteen from you now?" Jeff asks.

"Yeah, I'll go get it for you." He gets up and heads to the safe in the extra bedroom. He punches in the code and pulls out a half-kilo block, wraps it inside a T-shirt, and heads back out.

He passes it to Jeff. "Here, put this in your SUV."

Jeff takes the T-shirt and leaves to put it in his car. The girls come back a second after the door closes. "Where's Jeff?" Tanya asks.

"Oh, you forgot something in the car. He will be back in just one second," he responds.

Once Jeff returns, the couples hang out and drink at the house for an hour or two until Tanya says, "I'm tired, Jeff. Are you ready to go home?"

"Yes, I'm pretty tired, too. Let's go," Jeff responds. Tanya gives Courtney a hug and waves bye to him. Jeff and him shake hands. After Jeff and Tanya leave him and Courtney head back to the bedroom.

-----

His phone rings the next morning. "Hey, have you seen Jeff today?" Tanya asks from the other end.

"Nope, why? What's up?"

"He told me he had to do something this morning, and he would be back...and that was almost three hours ago."

*Jeff ain't like that...something had to have went wrong with that deal.*

"Have you called his phone?"

"Yes, and he won't answer," she replies as she softly begins to cry.

"Don't worry about him Tanya; he can take care of himself."

"I know..." she tries to respond, but he cuts her off midsentence.

"He is fine. He probably just forgot his cell in the car or something. He'll get ahold of us soon...but if he does call you, tell him to call me too, okay? I will talk to you later."

"Thanks again."

"No problem, Tanya," he responds and hangs up. The rest of the day continues as planned. He takes care of business, re-upping with Papi. He stops by a few places to drop off product and pick up money. A while after returning, he hears a knock at the front door. He is surprised when he opens the door and Tanya is standing in the doorway, crying hysterically.

"What's wrong, Tanya?" he asks as he brings her into the house and locks the door behind her.

She turns to him; a look of disbelief floods her features. "What do you mean, *what's wrong*? You haven't seen the news?" she replies.

"No I haven't, Ma. I've been busy all day. What's on the news?" She doesn't respond. She just keeps crying. "What is on the news, Tanya?" he asks again.

She looks at him with a terrifying, evil look in her eye. "He's on the news because he's fucking dead!" she yells. She keeps repeating this as she starts to hit him.

After a few minutes of wrestling around with her, he calms her down. "How did this happen?"

She continues to cry, breaking up the story into pieces, but mostly saying that Jeff was shot in his car. He drove himself to the hospital where he was later pronounced dead. She begins crying hysterically again. He tries to comfort her as she continues to cry, but he stays quiet.

A few minutes pass as he unwraps his arms from around her. His anger and frustration seep into one another. "Fuck!" he shouts.

She stares at him. "Do you know where he went today? Please Smurf, if you do know where he went, will you please tell me?"

He turns back to her. "He told me that he was going to meet a guy named Quick."

Her eyes open wide. "I gotta go…. I gotta go," she says in a frantic voice.

"Where you going?" he asks.

"I…I… I don't know… I just got to go." She hurries out the door and into her car before speeding off.

*For a girl that doesn't know where she's going, she sure seems to be going there pretty fast.*

-----

An hour passes before Tanya arrives at an old apartment building. Its weathered, brick exterior is checkered with window air-conditioning units.

*I'm going to kill this motherfucker when I see him.*

She enters the building and walks down the hallway toward apartment number eighteen.

She bangs hard on the door. "I know you're in here, Quick. Open the door!" she yells.

She hears movement from inside the apartment. The sound of the locks clicking send adrenaline through her veins, and she busts in to the apartment. She pulls out a chrome, .45 caliber pistol and aims it at Quick's face. "You have twenty seconds to tell me what I want to hear! Family or not, I will blow your fucking brains all over this apartment!" she yells, tears rolling down her face.

"Hey, hold on, Cousin! Just relax," he says, trying to calm her down.

"You have fifteen seconds."

He can tell by the sound of her voice that she is not playing. "Okay, okay, Tanya! I'll tell you everything...just put the gun down!" he pleads again.

"Ten seconds," she says as she cocks the hammer on the gun. "I want to know everything. Now!"

Okay, okay! I was with these two guys, Leo and Teddy...a couple of niggas I've been selling some shit to here and there. They came to me and wanted to buy an amount I didn't have, so I called Jeff to cover me!"

"Keep going," she says.

"Well we're down at the spot chilling, waiting for Jeff to show, and a black SUV rolls up slow, and before I could talk, they started unloading their guns into the truck... I didn't even know that was Jeff! I thought he would have a trap car to come meet in!"

"Did these people know you were meeting Jeff, or just someone?" she asks.

"No, only I knew Jeff was coming," he replies.

She shakes her head in disbelief. "Did they say anything? Names? Places? Anything?" she asks.

"I heard them say something about a dude named Smurf. I only heard that name though," he replies.

*Why would they say Smurf's name? Was he in on it? Was that bullet meant for him?*

The thoughts and emotions are tormenting her. "I'm willing to let you get away this time, but family or not--if I find out you're lying, I'm going to put one of these .45 caliber bullets in your head," she says as she makes her way to the door. She turns back one last time. "Keep your phone on and keep it next to you. If I call, you better answer."

-----

Smurf is already on the streets, doing his own investigating. While patrolling the blocks trying to find this dude named Quick, his anger builds. He can feel the dark mist filling his body. The same darkness that consumes him every time, before he takes a life.

*I'm going to kill this nigga when I find him. One for Jeff and two for making me search so long for him.*

He spots a woman on the corner and approaches her. "I'm looking for Quick; do you know where I can find him?"

The woman turns and points to a spot on the next corner up the road. "That's where you will find him, I think," she replies.

He doesn't ask more; he just goes where she points. He starts getting a twitch in his trigger hand as he feels the darkness creep into his eyes.

He spots a guy talking to what looks to be a black female in a car. As he gets closer to the car, he notices it's Tanya. "What the fuck!" he yells, drawing his gun from his waist.

She looks at him with his gun drawn. "Smurf, calm down!" she yells.

"You didn't help him kill Jeff, did you?" he yells.

"No! I love Jeff, and I'm going to take care of the problem, so go home!" she yells back.

"I swear Tanya, if I--"

She cuts him off midsentence. "Go home, Smurf! I got this! Trust me for once, will you? Please?" she says. Quick gets into her car, and they pull away, leaving him standing on the corner.

*What does she know that I don't know?*

-----

Later that night, Tanya and Quick pull up to the club. You better hope this is going to work," she says to him.

"Hey, you told me to get you introduced to them. Well...Teddy is busy, but Leo is here, and he's got a thing for pretty girls," Quick responds.

They enter the club and head towards the back. Quick spots Leo in the V.I.P section and nudges Tanya. "He's right over there." She looks at Leo, dressed in an academic outfit with braids in his hair and a pair of color-matching tennis shoes.

Quick leads her to her target. After Quick shakes his hand, he introduces Tanya to him. Leo eyes her up and down. She is dressed in a one-piece, red dress, showing off her large breasts and Coke-bottle frame.

"Hi," Tanya says.

"Hey, I'm Leo," he responds.

"I'm Tanya," she says. The only thing running through her mind is Jeff's dead body.

*This nigga better enjoy this night, because I'm gonna murk his ass later.*

They continue to party the night away at the club. She sticks close to Leo by dancing and grinding on him. She lets him rub his hands all over her. Each time he touches her, it makes her anger swell. It's not going to stop what she came here to do.

Another few hours pass, and the bar tender yells for last call. "You want to come back to my crib?" Leo asks.

"Actually, I'm from out of town, so I got a hotel room. You want to go?" she asks.

"Yeah let's go," Leo responds.

They leave the club and make their way to the hotel. While driving she asks, "You got a condom?"

"No," he responds.

"Well you ain't touching this without one."

"Okay, I'll stop and get some." They stop by a gas station and he runs inside to get some condoms.

*I hope this works.*

He returns after a few minutes with a box of condoms. "So which hotel are you staying at?"

"The Holiday Inn."

"Alright," he responds.

Once they arrive at the hotel, she grabs him by the hand. "Follow me." She leads him into the hotel through the back door and down the hallway to room 155.

"Just relax," she says as she pushes him onto the bed. She climbs on top of him and begins kissing him. She rubs her hands all over his chest, pulling off his shirt. She pushes him down and kisses his stomach, making her way down to his pants. She tugs his pants down and begins sucking his cock.

*Gotta do it good for this nigga since it's his last.*

She slides up and down with her mouth and licks the tip. He is now fully erect. She smacks it against the top of her bottom lip. "Looks like someone's ready to go."

"Come on, Ma, let's fuck."

She smiles. "I got to tell you something... I'm a freak. Do you think you can handle me?"

"Trust me, I can handle you," he responds.

"Well, I have a fetish," she says.

"What's that?"

"I like to tie up my guys while I ride them," she says as she continues to suck his cock.

"I don't know, Ma," he says nervously.

"Well, if you want this pussy, you have to let me handcuff you up, okay?"

He grins. "Okay, come on."

She gets up and goes into the bathroom, only to return with a pair of handcuffs. She puts the cuffs through a homemade hook that she made earlier. After cuffing both hands, she slides out of her red dress, revealing her natural breasts and bald pussy. She slides up his legs over his hard cock and puts her left breast in his mouth. She lets off a soft moan when she feels his tongue graze her nipple. "I like that."

She moans again as she smacks her ass. She opens up a condom, places it in her mouth and pushes it down until it is fully covering his cock. She straddles him again and slowly pushes the head and the shaft into her until he is balls-deep inside her. She begins riding him, her moans becoming more intense. The size of him is sending her over the edge. As she begins to orgasm, she continues to ride him.

She notices that he has his eyes closed from the sensations her tight pussy's giving him. She reaches under the pillow and grabs a roll of duct tape and places a strip across his mouth. He muffles in protest, but she rides him harder. She continues until the pulsating from inside her lets her know he reached orgasm. She then reaches her hand under the other side of the pillow and grabs a .22 caliber pistol and points it at his head. "This is for Jeff, you bitch-ass nigga."

She pulls the trigger.

# JJ

Over the next few months, things seem to go pretty good for JJ. His probation officer is cool and is very easy on him. His relationship with Stacy is great, and the projects he works on with George continue to produce a decent amount of money.

One night, while working to make a fairly large batch of THC liquid, George turns and looks at him. "Hey, JJ?"

"Yes," he replies as he continues to work.

"Hey, I've been doing some research on that MDMA powder."

JJ stops what he's doing and turns to look at George.

*I got him.*

"What about it, George?" he asks.

"Well, I figured out what we need...but it's going to take at least forty-eight hours to do it... We would need a lab outside of here."

He places his hand on his head as he tries to think of possible locations. "Does it have to be really well ventilated?... Can we maybe do this at my house in my bedroom?"

"Well JJ, the room *does* need to be ventilated...but since we wouldn't be doing a lot, we could probably do it in your apartment."

"Okay, that's great! You still have that formula I gave you, George?"

"Yeah, it's at home."

"Alright, good...so, when do you want to do this?"

"That's totally up to you, JJ. I figure we might as well try and do this. The only way we can do better is by trying to find a storage space.

He smiles. "George, ain't that the truth! Do you still have the glassware that we got from our kits... The one we had to buy at the beginning of the year for class?"

"Yeah I do," George replies.

"Okay, well, tomorrow bring the glassware to my house and, we'll set it up and go get all the chemicals we need to do this."

"Okay...we're still splitting the profits, right?" George asks.

"Yes, we split half the cost and half the profits," he replies.

"Okay...I just wanted to make sure," George replies. They continue to finish the THC liquid before packing everything up and heading home.

The next day, he wakes up and finds Mark sitting on the couch. "What's up, Mark?" he asks.

"Shit, nothing," Mark replies.

He sits down in the chair across from Mark. "Hey Mark, I have a question for you about that powder MDMA."

"What is it?" Mark asks.

"Is it pretty good? Do you think it will sell fast?"

"Are you serious, JJ? That stuff is clean as hell! Roll hard and go to bed, then wake up the next day with no hangover!" Mark responds.

"Okay, well this doesn't leave me and you...and what I'm about to tell you does not leave this apartment... You understand me?"

"Yeah, yeah. I hear you," Mark replies.

"Well, I'm going to set up a lab in the apartment and make a few batches of that MDMA powder.... So, that means no one, I mean *no one*, comes in this house other than you, George, and myself."

"George? George, the kid from your chemistry class?" Mark says in a confused voice.

"Yes, that George...but keep this on the down-low. I do not need anyone finding this out... even Stacy," he replies.

"Alright, alright, my lips are sealed," Mark says as he motions an invisible zipper across his lips.

"Okay good." He gets up and walks towards his room. He stops just before his door. "Oh, by the way, Mark..."

"Yeah, JJ?"

"We start today. So no one in the house."

"Okay, nobody in the house, starting today," Mark repeats.

JJ enters his room and closes the door. He picks up his phone to text George.

**Hey bro when are you coming over?**

While waiting for a response, he takes a shower and gets ready for the day. An hour later, he finally gets a reply.

Hey JJ sorry I just woke up. I'll be over in about an hour

**Okay I will see when you get here**

He presses SEND and gets on his computer. The continuing thought of a super drug keeps racing through his mind. He hasn't even created it, and he's already addicted. The vibration of his phone interrupts his research. Another text from George.

Open your door.

*It hasn't been an hour already, has it?*

He looks down at his watch. "Damn! It's been almost two hours!"

He hurries to the door and unlocks it. "Hey, JJ! Sorry I'm late!" George says.

"It's cool! Let's just put the stuff in the living room," he replies as he points towards the living room. "You brought that formula, didn't you George?"

"Yeah, I have it," George responds as he pulls the paper out of his backpack. "Yeah, this formula isn't too hard. We can definitely get all these chemicals from your self-home-and-lawn-care businesses. We *do* need to go to a photo shop place though, because one chemical is hard to find...but a lot of it is in a certain photo liquid."

"Okay George, how much do you think it's gonna cost us?"

"Well, if my math is correct, for the formula and the cost of the products we would pay roughly $1 per pill...and I believe with the formula we can make 2,000 pills...so it's going to cost us $1,000 each today."

"Okay George, do you have your $1,000?"

Yeah, got mine."

"Okay, let's go." They leave the apartment to begin the process of obtaining the chemicals. They bounce from different home-and-lawn-care-service businesses as well as a couple photo shops. They return six hours later with everything they need.

"Where we can set up the glassware, JJ?" George asks.

"We can put it up right here," he replies.

"Well, JJ, we can, I guess... Why is it out in the open by the door?" George says nervously.

"Hey, Man, we just need to knock out two or three batches...then we can rent a place and just set up in that," he replies.

"Alright, JJ, that's fine. Let's just set up here...but what about your roommate? Does he know?

"Yeah, I told him to not bring anyone here."

"Okay, well let's get started." They set up all the glassware on the tables and TV stand. "Now we just follow the formula." They begin to mix the chemicals. JJ opens the window, but leaves the blinds down.

Over the next few days it's a waiting game. And more mixing. The exact amount at the exact time. Precision.

They take turns watching and following the formula. The last hours come, and they sit nervously, waiting to see if they did it right. As the product finally crystallizes, they watch it to make sure the purity is at its best.

After five washes, they are left with about thirteen ounces of beautiful, pearl-white and sparkly powder. "So we test it?" George asks.

"We try it," he confirms with a smile.

"I don't know about that JJ..."

"Well *we're* not going to try it... We need to find a guinea pig to try it."

"Yeah, that sounds a lot better."

"Okay. Well, I'll get Mark to try it." He gets up and walks over to Mark's room and bangs on the door.

"What's up?" Mark yells through the door.

"Come out here!" he yells back.

Mark comes out into the living room. "What's going on here?"

"Mark, snort this," he says as he hands the powder from his digital scale to him. "It's 200 milligrams of the finished product." Mark smiles. He rolls up some paper and snorts the powder. JJ looks at George. "Now we wait."

"Hey Mark, did it burn at all?" George asks.

"Not really...but it's bitter... I can taste it dripping down my throat."

JJ looks at George. "Bitter is good, George. That's how you know if it's good."

"Ah, okay...well, that's a plus! Well, while we wait, JJ, let's get this place cleaned up."

JJ turns to Mark. "Hey Bro, go chill out for a little bit and let us get this cleaned up." Mark nods and heads back to his room.

After about an hour of cleaning, they check on Mark. They walk into his room to find him lying on his bed, listening to music. "Hey Mark, you feeling anything?" he asks.

Mark turns and looks at him with a lost look on his face. "What did you say?"

"Oh shit...you're fucked up, aren't you?"

Mark just smiles. "Man, this shit hit me like a semi... I mean everything...the lights...the...sounds...the sensations...it's all pulsating through my body!"

JJ looks at George with a grin. "We did it, George! We did it!" They both smile and clap hands. "I believe it's time to celebrate!"

-----

The next few batches sell faster than the first. Mark can't get it out fast enough. Even Leon is buying from them. Just like that, the supplier becomes the customer.

One afternoon George, Stacy and JJ are sitting at the apartment. "I think we need a vacation," he says.

"Where to?" Stacy asks.

"I don't know… How about Chicago? We'll go party out there with some friends of mine from back home… What do you think?"

"Sure, we need to get away and enjoy ourselves," George replies.

"Yeah, that will be fun!" Stacy says.

"Alright, so we will go down this weekend and come back on Monday," he says.

"How much money do we need to take?" George asks.

"Don't worry about it. I'll take care of the weekend."

The next few days feel like months as they wait in anticipation. He calls his parents. "Hey, mom."

"Hi, Honey!"

"Mom, I just called to let you know me and a couple of friends are coming home this weekend."

"Okay, that's great! Your dad and I will have the house ready!"

"Okay, thank you! I just wanted to call and tell you. I'll see you and dad later. I love you."

"I love you too, Honey," his mom replies before he disconnects.

While packing up his clothes, he goes into his shoebox and grabs one large stack of money. It's roughly $3,000 in $50s and $20s. He also grabs ten plastic-gel-cap, molly pills that he had weighed and filled with their MDMA molecule powder.

*My boys back home are going to love this!*

He puts the pills in a bottle and buries them deep in his suitcase.

The next day, they all meet at his apartment before they leave. He drops two ounces of powder off in Mark's room and writes a note.

Hope this is enough!

-JJ

He signs it and places the baggy on top of the note. They make one last stop at the gas station before heading off to Chicago.

"How long is it to Chicago?" George asks from the backseat.

"It's between six and seven hours," he replies.

"Oh, well, I'm going to sleep then," George replies as he leans his head back. They continue to drive, only stopping once at the Iowa/Illinois border to fill up with gas.

By the time they reach Chicago, both Stacy and George are sleeping. "Hey guys, wake up! We are here!" he says. Stacy and George slowly wake and look at the skyline. They drive on the freeway towards his parents' home on the north side of Chicago.

"Damn! These houses are huge!" Stacy says as they pull off into his neighborhood.

"Yeah, JJ, these houses are pretty big," George replies from the back.

He just smiles and pulls in the driveway. "Here it is. This is my house."

"Wow, JJ, this house looks like an old castle!" George says.

"Yeah! With that big, gray brick and old Victorian style...it's like a mansion!" Stacy says.

He honks his horn as he slows to a stop. His mom and dad walk out to meet them. "Hi, Mom. Hi, Dad."

"Hey, Honey! How was the trip? You run into a lot of traffic?" his mom asks in an excited voice.

Their arms open for a hug. "Gosh, I've missed you!" his mom says, squeezing him in a hug.

"I've missed you too, Mom," he replies.

"Hello, Jeremy," his dad says.

"Hi, Dad," he replies.

"Come on, give your dad a hug!"

They hug for a moment, and he takes a step back. "I want to introduce my friends. This is George."

"Hi, Mr. and Mrs. Jepenski." They both smile and nod.

"And this is my girlfriend, Stacy."

"Oh my gosh... I'm so happy to finally meet you!" his mom says as she hugs Stacy.

"Nice to meet you, Stacy," his dad says as he shakes her hand.

"It's nice to finally meet the both of you, as well," she responds.

"Come on, let's get you guys settled. We're making dinner... It is almost finished," his mom says as she grabs Stacy's hand and guides her along inside.

After getting settled, everyone sits down around the dinner table. "Mr. and Mrs. Jepenski, you have a beautiful home," Stacy says.

His mother giggles. "Oh, thank you, Stacy," she replies.

"So, what are you kids going to do this weekend? I know you didn't come to hang out with us old people," his dad says in a joking manner.

"Hey! We aren't old!" his mom responds as she punches her husband in the arm.

"Well, I figured I could bring these guys to see the city...visit you guys and see some old friends for a weekend," he replies.

"That sounds like fun!" his mom says. "Where you guys from?"

"Well, Mrs.Jepenski, I'm from Nevada, Iowa. It's a small town in the northern part of Iowa," Stacy responds.

His mom nods and looks at George. "How about you, George...where are you from?"

"Well, I'm from Aurora, Colorado. It's next to Denver."

"Ah, I know exactly where that is! I know that's a nice area in Colorado... I've done business there. So, what are your plans for tonight? Do you have any?" his dad chimes in.

"Well, I was planning to take these guys to the clubs and probably call a few of the guys and go hang out with them, too."

"That sounds like fun, but remember JJ... What do we always tell you?"

"Don't drink and drive," he responds.

"Yes, please don't... The police are getting very strict these days," Dad warns.

"Okay, Dad, we'll have a designated driver tonight," he replies. His dad just nods his head and starts eating his food.

"Hey, you kids better eat before the food gets cold," his mom says.

*This is going to be one hell of a weekend...one hell of a weekend.*

# TANYA

She stands and watches the fire engulf the hotel room where Leo's dead body remains. All she can do is smile. "Now, that one was for Jeff, Nigga," she says under her breath.

She calmly makes her way down the hallway, trying to go unnoticed. She gets in her car and speeds away. She cruises down the street with her window down and her hair blowing in the wind. Her thoughts wander to memories of her childhood.

She grew up around gangsters. Her mom was black, and her dad was Colombian. She was picked on a lot, but her older brother protected her. Her family was super close. They all watched over each other and protected one another. Her father taught her how to survive in the world. She was taught by playing games. Little did she know, those games would create the woman she is today.

She grew up in the shadows of her older brother, which kept her eyes off the family business. All she knew was she was daddy's little girl, and whatever she wanted, she got. Price meant nothing to her. As she grew older, the boys and girls that picked on her became afraid of her, which made her suspicious.

One day, while riding with her dad, she noticed something odd. Most little girls wouldn't pay attention, but she was not like most little girls. Sitting in the car that cloudy day, she learned about drug trafficking. After seeing her first drug deal happen, all she could do was think about her father. The loving man who gave her anything she ever wanted. Now, she knew how he did it.

The day went by, and she didn't say anything to her father about what she saw. As the weeks passed, her attitude changed, ever so slightly. Eventually, she slowly became a female gangster.

One pain-filled night, while she was out shopping with her older brother, Mario, he was gunned down in a drive-by shooting. She watched him take his last breath. The event pushed her over the edge.

She needed revenge.

Later that night, she cried to her father. "I want them to die, Daddy! I just want them to die!"

Her father held her close and whispered in his little girl's ear. "I swore I'd give you what you want in life...and if that's what you want, then you will get it." Without knowing it, she had set up her first hit. Just one of many in her life.

The day of Mario's funeral was the day that changed her life forever. The purity in her heart and soul left her forever as she watched her brother's casket lower into the ground. She took a vow that day: anyone who messed with her family would be dealt with by her.

A few weeks passed, and emotions started to settle down. On a gloomy night, she saw her dad sitting in his office. "Dad?" she asked

"Hi, Honey. Come in here."

"I have a question, Dad."

"Okay, Honey, what is it?"

"Do you sell drugs?"

"What? Who told you that?" he replies in an angry voice.

"Dad, I'm not dumb... I notice things," she answers.

Her dad shakes his head and gets up. "Honey, sit down." She sits down on the chair across the table from him. "Sometimes, Honey, people have opportunities to do great things in life...like play sports, be a CEO of a big business, or even an inventor... I was given the opportunity to do great things, but on a different level."

She looks at him with an emotionless face. "Is that why Mario died, Dad?"

Her dad leans forward and places his hands on the table between them. "Honey, your brother was involved in things that I was unaware of... If I knew it, I could have prevented it."

"I want to help, Dad."

Her dad chuckles. "Honey, you're not going to get involved in this stuff. I won't allow it."

-----

Over the next few years, Tanya starts working to prove to her father what she's capable of. She proves her worth in the family business by selling, collecting, and working out logistics.

One night, her father calls her into his office. "Yes, Dad?" she replies as she walks in.

"Sit down, Honey."

She sits. "What's up, Dad?"

"Since the conversation we had after your brother's death, you've been trying to prove to me that you can survive in this dog-eat-dog world...and you finally proved to me that even as a female, you scare most men."

"Okay...so what are you saying, Dad?"

"I'm saying I will let you into this family business, but the first time it gets too hot, you're done... I can't lose another child to this game."

She places her hand over her heart. "I swear...when it gets too much."

She has no idea that she would outlive even her loving father when it comes to this game.

As time progresses, she puts fear into the men in her life. She's Daddy's little girl, known for her very short temper, lack of emotion and very talented trigger finger. When there's a problem in the business, her father calls on her to correct it. Because of her smarts and ninja-like movements, she can be in and out, and no one would even know what happened.

The next few months pass. She starts taking small steps up the business ladder. It doesn't start until after her first kill. On a weekday afternoon, she receives a phone call from her dad. "Hello?" she says.

"Hey, Tanya, Honey...I need to see you."

"When? Where?" she asked.

"In the next hour or so. We need to discuss something. Meet me down at the restaurant."

"Okay, I'll see you soon."

After getting dressed, she leaves for the family restaurant. It's a

Columbian restaurant, Nothing special, just a run down restaurant. Secretly owned, of course. She enters the restaurant and heads towards the back where two bodyguards wait. "Hey guys," she says.

"Hello, Tanya," one of them says as he opens the door for her.

She walks in, and her father greets her. "Hello, Honey."

"Hi, Daddy," she replies as she walks up and gives him a kiss on the cheek. "What did you need to talk about?"

"Well, we have a problem with the family."

"What do you mean, Daddy? A problem with the family?"

"Well, there are reasons to believe that someone in the family has been selling us out to our competition."

"So, what do you need from me?"

"We need you to take care of the problem."

"Who is it?" she asks.

"Chapo," her father responds.

"Chapo? Are you sure? He's always been your good friend, Daddy."

"I know honey, but I guess he felt he didn't need to be loyal to me anymore."

"So, when you want it done?"

"Soon...very soon. Do it how you want, just make it look like an accident."

"Okay," she nods in understanding. "Is there anything else you need?"

"No, Honey, you go. I love you."

"I love you too, Daddy," she says as she leaves.

*I wonder how I'm going to murk Chapo.*

Over the next few days, she tails Chapo on his daily routine. She follows him everywhere, and soon begins to notice a pattern. "Man, this guy really likes the strip club," she says out loud as she follows him into the parking lot.

Once inside, she scans her surroundings.

*This place ain't too bad...a couple of stripper stages, glass tables, black chairs, a V.I.P section, a private dance area and a full bar.*

She makes her way to the bar and orders a drink, keeping a sly eye on Chapo. After a few minutes, she watches him approach a young lady. The woman takes his hand and leads him to the V.I.P area.

*That's how I'll get him. I'll poison his drink...make it look like a heart attack.*

She plays the event out in her head, setting the plans for how she'll do it. She leaves the club and stops by a friend of the family's to get what she needs.

The next day, she follows the plan with precision. She won't be caught slipping.

She arrives at the strip club twenty minutes before Chapo and begins preparation. The time passes until Chapo walks right into the trap. She tells the bartender to mix two drinks, while a dancer distracts Chapo, just as Tanya paid her to do. Tanya drops a pinch of a white, powdery substance into both glasses, just to be on the safe side.

*This better work.*

She slides away undetected and moves to the end of the bar, allowing her to view the V.I.P entrance. She watches him enter the area and waits for a female scream, letting her know the job is complete. A few minutes later, a loud scream comes from the back room.

*It's done. Daddy will be proud of me.*

She slips out the front door to her car and drives away. She pulls out her phone and calls her dad.

"Hello?" he answers.

"Hi, Daddy. I took the trash out for the garbage people."

"Okay, Honey, thank you. I got to get going, though. I will see you at home, okay?"

"Okay, Daddy, I will see you later," she responds.

The rest of the day passes as she lies on the couch watching TV. The news comes on, and the TV anchor begins speaking. "Welcome back. Now for our latest story... Two men have been found dead at a local gentleman's club..." A picture of Chapo and another Mexican national named Juan Guzman appear on the screen.

"Oh shit!" she says out loud.

*I killed Juan... He's the son of Drug Lord, Marco Guzman!*

Her father enters the living room. "Tanya?" he says.

"Yeah, Dad?"

"I need to talk to you."

"What is it?"

"Did you know Juan was there?"

She shakes her head. "No Sir, I didn't see him at all."

"Hmm..." He takes a second to think. "Well, you remember our talk about if it gets too hot, you'll stop?"

"Yes, Sir."

"Well, I think it's time you take a break."

"What? Why?" she shouts. "I'll fix it... It was an accident!"

"This is going to start a war between our families, and I need you to be safe, Honey."

"Hello!" a manly voice says from the front of the house. They both turn as Papi, her uncle, walks through the living room. Once in the living room, Papi greets his brother and his niece. "Hey, Albert?" Papi says.

"Yes, Papi?" her father responds.

Papi eyes Tanya. "Can I talk to you in private?"

"Yeah, let's go into my office." They leave her sitting in the living room.

As they enter the office, Albert closes the door behind them. "What's going on, Papi?"

"You know about Juan?"

"Yes...what about it?" he asks.

"Well, word on the street is that we did it."

He snorts. "There's no proof that we did it!"

"Yeah, Albert, I know what you mean...but they're the type of fucked up family that will act first, *then* ask questions later."

"So what you think we should do?"

"Prepare for the worst...hope for the best," Papi responds.

"Okay, Papi… I need something from you…a promise."

"Anything, Brother, what is it?" Papi asks.

"If anything happens to me, take care of my little girl… Promise me you'll take care of my little girl, and you will keep her safe."

Papi nods. "I promise, Albert."

"Thank you… Now, Papi, since we got problems, let's try to set up a meeting…have a sit down with Marco. Also, send Tanya somewhere for a while until things cool down and everything blows over…maybe down to Miami, to her aunt's house. She has some family her age down there."

"Alright, Albert. I'll get her on the next flight out of here," Papi responds.

They both come out of the office to find Tanya sitting on the couch. She looks up. "Everything okay, Daddy?"

"Yeah, Tanya, it's going to be okay."

"Good," she responds.

"Hey, Honey?"

"Yeah?"

"Hey, I'm going to send you and Mom down to your aunt's for a while."

"What? Why? I won't leave you, Daddy!" she yells.

"Tanya!" he yells back. "I don't know what I would do if something happened to you or your mother...so, go to Miami. Enjoy it! Spend some time with your little cousins, Mindy and Alex...and just relax."

She begins crying. Her dad places his thumbs under her eyes and wipes away her tears. "Look at me, Tanya." She sniffles as she tries to look her dad in his eyes. "You're always going to be Daddy's little girl, Honey," he says.

"I know, but--" She gets cut off by her father hugging her. Not another word is said about the situation.

The next day, she is shuttled to the airport with her mother and flown to Miami on a private jet.

Once in Miami, all she can do is think about her father and how she started all this drama.

"Tanya! Tanya!" Mindy yells.

Tanya, spaced out in the daydream, realizes her cousin is yelling at her. "What? I'm sorry," Tanya says.

"You okay, Cousin? Were you daydreaming?" Mindy asks.

Yeah, I'm fine. Come on, let's go to the beach and lay out!"

Within a short time, the two of them are laying out on the white sands of Miami Beach. She puts a fake smile on her face. Something is wrong, she can feel it.

At the end of the night she receives a call from Papi, telling her of her father's death at the family restaurant. Tears fill her eyes. She knew there was something wrong. She didn't want to leave Chicago, but she promised her dad. Now her father is dead. She feels so helpless. She could have stopped it...

"Hey, Tanya?" Papi says gently.

"Yes, Papi?"

"You need to break the news to your mom...and you both need to come home now."

"Okay," she replies as she hangs up.

Mindy walks up slowly to her cousin. "Are you okay?"

Tanya catches her breath before speaking. "No Mindy, I'm not. My father was just killed back home in Chicago..."

"OH MY GOD! I'm so sorry!" Mindy replies as she puts her arm around Tanya and comforts her. "If I can do anything, let me know." Tears fill Mindy's eyes.

"Come with me, Mindy."

"Come with you where?"

"To Chicago."

"Tanya, to Chicago? Are you serious? They got snow up there!"

Tanya begins to laugh. "Shut up, Mindy."

"Well, that's good, Cousin...you still have a little sense humor," Mindy replies with a smile. "How long you need me to be up there?"

"I'm not sure Mindy, but you'll probably be staying with me for a while. So...please come to Chicago with me?" she asks as she wipes the tears off her face.

"Okay, Cousin, you got me...let's go!"

# JJ

"So, where do you guys want to go?" JJ asks as the three of them sit around in his parents' living room.

"Take us to one of your favorite spots," Stacy says.

"Yeah, you're from here…just show us a good time!" George replies.

"Okay, we will go to Biology Bar."

"Okay! Since it's picked, I'm going to go get ready," Stacy says as she gets up and heads towards the stairs that lead to JJ's room."

"You better get ready too," he says to George.

"Yeah, you are probably right… I better go get ready," George replies as he gets up and heads towards the guest bedroom.

JJ pulls out his cell and begins a mass text.


**Hey everyone I'm back for the weekend! I'm heading down to biology bar tonight so come party with me. V.I.P bottle service**


After closing his cell and placing it back in his pocket, he heads up the stairs to his old bedroom.

Once inside his room, he finds Stacy in a bra and panties doing her makeup in the connected bathroom.

He slowly walks up behind her and begins kissing her neck, softly.

"Hey, now," she says.

"What? I can't kiss you?" he replies.

"What if your parents catch us?" she responds.

"They won't come in, don't worry about that," he says as he slowly slips her bra straps down her shoulders.

As he continues to kiss her neck, he watches her in the mirror. He gently pulls her bra down, revealing her luscious, natural breasts. He begins lightly tugging and twisting both nipples, feeling them grow between his fingertips.

"Mmmm," she says as she lets off a soft moan. He spins her around and lifts her onto the bathroom counter. He continues kissing her and starts slowly making his way down to the hidden pearl between her legs. "Oh my..." she moans as he spreads her legs.

He pulls her panties to the side, pulls her pussy lips apart and begins licking in a circular motion on her swollen clit. She grabs his hair as she begins to gyrate her hips to the motion of his tongue. While continuing to lick her swollen clit, he undoes his pants with his left hand

and pulls them down, revealing his hard cock. He switches hands and begins to slowly play with himself. As he does this, she starts to shake, her climax creeping closer.

"Oh fuck," she moans as she bites on her hand.

Now completely erect, he sweeps up between her legs and pushes his cock deep inside her. She lets off a deep moan and arches her back. He continues to pump her fast and hard. She pulls him close, wrapping her legs around him and pushing him deeper with every pump. She begins moaning into his mouth as they kiss. The thrusts begin to send shivers up her spine.

"I'm going to come," he moans in her ear.

"Yeah baby, come for me," she replies.

He lets off a few more deep moans before he pulls out and finishes all over her stomach and upper legs. She takes his cock in her hand and slowly massages it, getting all of his semen out, then licks the tip clean. She swallows, then kisses the head of his cock. "Now get out so I can get ready," she says with a smile.

He smiles back as he pulls up his pants and leaves the bathroom. He changes clothes and grabs a large wad of cash out of his luggage.

Before closing up the bag, he grabs the MDMA powder pills and puts them into his jeans pocket.

After finishing up, they meet George down in the living room. "You guys ready to go?" he asks.

Both Stacy and George nod in agreement. "Alright, let's go," he replies.

They end up at Biology Bar about an hour later. "God, this line is long as hell," Stacy says in a pouty voice.

"Don't worry, you guys, come with me," he replies. They make their way towards the front of the line.

"Hey, you got to wait," the lead security says. JJ leans in and begins whispering into the man's ear, and then reaches into his pocket and pulls out what looks to be nothing and shakes the man's hand.

The security nods as he lets them pass.

"What did you say to that guy?" Stacy asks.

"I told him I had $200 for him if he let us get in. He agreed, so I paid the man." They make their way to the bar and order drinks. The crowd is popping; the club is packed full of kids their age.

As George and Stacy look around the club, he sends another mass text. A few minutes later he receives a response.

VIP come now.

He puts away his phone and grabs Stacy's hand. "Come on, let's go," he says as he leads them back towards the V.I.P tables.

"Yo, JJ!" a voice yells from a booth. A young man with dirty blonde hair and an average build greets them. He's dressed in a long-sleeved, button-down shirt and black slacks.

"Hey, Petey! How's my boy doing?" he says to Petey as they briefly hug.

"Hey, JJ! Who are your friends?"

"Well Petey, this is my girlfriend, Stacy, and this is my boy, George."

Both Stacy and George greet Petey with a handshake. JJ asks the waitress to bring back a few bottles of vodka. As soon as the bottles are dropped off, he makes everyone a drink. He makes something special for Stacy. He pulls out a gel-cap and dumps the contents into her drink. He then begins to mix it and hands it to her.

"Here you go, Stacy. I made this special for you," he whispers in her ear as he hands her the drink. He turns and looks at George. "Are you having fun?"

"Yeah, it's alright," George responds.

He turns back and whispers into Stacy's ear again. "Think you can help find George a date for tonight?"

She nods and grabs George's hand. "Come on, let's go dance."

George looks at him. He just nods and smiles. Stacy and George head to the dance floor while he and Petey begin catching up.

"So Petey, what are you up to these days?"

"I'm still at the University of Chicago, but just partying mostly. What about you?" Petey asks.

"Same shit. I'm still at ISU, and I party a lot as well."

"You still popping those pills?" Petey asks.

He begins to laugh. "Yes, what about you?"

"Well, here and there...not as much as I used to. It's been really hard finding good ones around here lately."

Petey's response is like music to JJ's ears. "No good pills, huh?"

"Not really, JJ...mostly just a bunch of bunk pills or really speedy pills and nothing worth taking."

JJ reaches into his pocket and pulls out one of his pills. "Here try this, I got a few."

Petey throws the pill in his mouth and washes it down with his drink. "If these are good, you have anymore?"

"I got enough, Petey."

"How much?"

"$15 or $10 each, but you have to buy all of them."

"Well JJ, we will see how this one is, and I'll let you know."

A few songs play, and Stacy returns with George and another girl. She looks to be of Colombian descent with black hair, brown eyes, dressed in a miniskirt and T-shirt.

"What's going on, guys?" he asks Stacy as she runs up to him and gives him a hug. A huge smile is plastered on her face. "Oh shit...you're fucked up, huh?" he asks her. She doesn't answer, but continues to smile. He smiles and turns his attention to George. "Hey, George, who is this with you? Are you not going to introduce me?"

"JJ, this is Mindy. Mindy, this is my friend, JJ."

"Nice to meet you, JJ," Mindy says.

He sticks out his hand and greets her. "The pleasure is all mine." He turns back to George. "Hey George, pour your girl a drink."

"Alright," George replies.

About forty-five minutes pass, and Stacy is getting antsy to dance. After tugging on his arm for a few minutes, he finally gives in. "Okay Stacy, let's dance." They vanish off to the dance floor.

After a couple of songs play, Petey joins them. "Hey bro," Petey says into his ear.

"What's up? You feeling it?" he asks.

"Okay, I'm fucked, Bro... Best roll I've had in months!"

"Well, that's good, enjoy it!" he replies.

"Oh I am, but the reason why I found you... I talked to some friends, and they want some, too... Do you have ten?"

"No, I got eight left."

"Okay, can I get them?"

"Yeah," he says as he reaches into his pocket. He pulls out the remaining pills and hands them to Petey. "I need $80 for those, Petey."

"Alright, okay, I got you... Give me like ten minutes." Petey leaves, and they continue dancing.

Finally, after dancing for half an hour straight, JJ and Stacy make their way back to the V.I.P area to relax. They join back up with George, Mindy, Petey and his friends.

Petey pulls out four $20 bills and hands them to him. "Thanks again, Bro," Petey says.

"No problem," he replies.

"Man, it's getting close to the end of the night... What are you guys going to do tomorrow?" Petey asks.

"I don't know. I was going to take them downtown and walk around," he responds.

"Well if you do, hit me up. I'll meet up with you guys," Petey replies.

He nods and turns to George and Stacy. "Are you guys ready to go?"

They both agree, but George seems reluctant. "I guess we can leave," he says in an unhappy voice.

"Well, George, get Mindy's number, and we will try to meet up with her tomorrow."

George, unfamiliar with women, smiles nervously and turns to Mindy to get her number. After the club, they head back to his house and sleep for the night.

The next morning, after everyone has showered and changed, he tells George to call Mindy. "See if she would like to go to lunch with us."

"Okay," George replies as he gets up and leaves the room.

"What are we going to do today?" Stacy asks.

"I think I'll take you guys downtown and walk around," he replies.

George returns and says, "She said to just call her when we get to wherever were going, and she will meet us."

"Okay, well let's finish eating, and then we will go." They finish and head downtown as planned.

While walking around they find the Hard Rock Café. "Hey let's go there," Stacy says.

"Okay, let's go there and get some drinks," he agrees. He looks at George. "Hey George, call Mindy and tell her to meet us here." George pulls out his phone and proceeds to call Mindy. JJ pulls out his phone.

"Who are you calling?" Stacy asks.

"Petey, to see how he's doing. And telling him to meet us down here."

After a few rings, Petey answers. "Hello?"

"Hey Petey, how are you feeling today?"

"Pretty good, actually! I don't even really feel like I partied last night... What are you guys up to?"

"Well, we are downtown and about to go eat at the Hard Rock. I called to see if you wanted to come."

"When?"

"Right now. We were going to have a few drinks first to wait for you."

"Okay, I'll be there in about twenty minutes."

"Okay, see you soon," he responds and hangs up. They enter the restaurant and head for a booth.

After about forty-five minutes, everyone is in the booth and ordering food.

After eating, they all decide to go walk around downtown Chicago. It's a beautiful, partly-cloudy day. Mindy, George and Stacy walk in front while JJ trails behind with Petey. The two slow down a bit to gain more distance. "Hey, JJ, I wanted to ask you something," Petey whispers.

"What's up, Man?"

"That stuff was good last night... You get that all the time?"

"When it's around I get it...why?"

"I'm asking, because everything here has been junk lately, and I could definitely unload that here for good money."

"Okay, but how would you get it here...transport wise...because I'm not bringing it."

"Well, I heard one of my guys talking about how they do weed and other stuff. What they do is vacuum seal it and hide it in stuff and mail it to P.O. boxes."

"No one has gotten caught yet?" he asks.

"No, they got it down to a science, Bro. Send it from a fake address to a P.O. box. They will never figure it out."

"I don't know, Petey...that sounds kind of fishy to me."

"Well, see if you can meet someone that works in the mailing business...maybe FedEx or whatever... to mail it for you. Pay him a few hundred dollars per package to make sure it gets sent. Put a fake address on it, and I'll send cash back to the address. Just have him hang onto it when it arrives."

"I don't know any people at them places, Petey."

"You're in college, Bro... There has to be at least one college kid that works at them places...and what's one thing college kids want? Money."

"Well, I'll see what I can do...but I can't promise anything," he responds.

"Well, if you do then let me know, because I'll get some from you."

He hears Mindy from the front of the group. "What are you guys going to do tonight?"

At that, everyone turns to JJ. "We don't have any plans for tonight. Do you know of something going on?" he asks Mindy.

"Well, my girls and I usually go to Secrets on Saturday nights. We're regulars down there, so no worries about the line to get in. Plus, they have a party tonight with a few popular DJs."

"Who are they?" Stacy asks.

"These guys are from Iowa. They got Ya Boy Dru Soy, DJ Bigboii, and Pri Yon Joni. They are part of the I-Party Crew!"

"Oh, that sounds like a lot of fun! What you think, JJ?" Stacy asks.

He shrugs. "It doesn't matter to me. What do you think, George?"

George nods. "I'm game!"

"Okay, Mindy, looks like we'll be there!"

"Okay, great!" Mindy says with a smile.

"Do they have V.I.P?" he asks.

"Yeah they do...do you want a table?"

"Yeah, get one with four bottles."

"Okay, I'll tell my friend. What type of bottles?"

"Vodka. I don't really like anything else." He looks to the others. "Is it okay with you guys?"

"Yeah, that's fine," they agree.

"Okay, so one table and four bottles of vodka. I'll text them in a minute," Mindy replies.

"You coming, Petey?" he asks.

"I'm not going to miss hanging out with my boy while he's in town! I'll be there," Petey responds.

-----

While changing at JJ's, George receives a text from Mindy.

Hey text when you get here. I'll meet you outside. Also I forgot-no tennis shoes and no t-shirts!

George closes his phone and continues getting dressed. He is the first one ready. Once JJ and Stacy are done, he stands. "How do I look?"

"You look good in the polo shirt and jeans...but why aren't you wearing tennis shoes?" Stacy asks.

"Oh, I forgot! Mindy texted me, and we can't wear T-shirts or tennis shoes."

"Oh, I'll be right back then," JJ says as he takes off toward his room.

He returns a few minutes later. "You guys ready?"

"Yeah," she says.

"Yeah man, let's go!" George says in an excited voice.

After leaving the house, they arrive down at the club. "That's a cool

sign!" Stacy says, pointing at the large, red-lettered SECRETS sign.

"Hey, text Mindy and tell her we are here."

George flashes a smile. "I'm ahead of you, JJ... I already sent it!"

Within moments, Mindy steps from behind the front doors in a

tight, one-piece dress. "Over here, guys!" she yells as she waves them

down. As they make their way closer, they see her talking to the

bouncer. She kisses the man on the cheek and turns to them. "Come on

guys, follow me," she says.

She leads them into the club. She turns slightly to speak, but keeps

moving forward. "It's at about 75% capacity... There's a lot of people,

but still room to move around."

"This is pretty cool with the bars on both sides of the club...

Where's the V.I.P?" Stacy asks.

"Yeah, it's pretty nice! They even take pictures where we first came in at, but the V.I.P is in the back past the dance floor," Mindy replies. She leads them to their table, where four vodka bottles sit waiting. After a few drinks, Mindy and George disappear off to the dance floor, while JJ and Stacy continue drinking. JJ's cell vibrates against his leg. He pulls it out to see a text from Petey.

Hey I'm here, come get me!

"Shit," he says as he reads the text.

"What, JJ? What's wrong?" she asks.

"Petey is here, but Mindy has to go get him."

"Oh...well go get her then!"

"Okay, I'll be right back."

He makes his way through the crowds and finds the couple dancing. "Hey guys, sorry to bother you, but Petey is outside... Can you please get him in?"

"Yeah, that's not a problem! I'll go get him and bring him to the V.I.P table."

"Okay, thank you," he responds as Mindy speeds off to retrieve

Petey. JJ and George head back towards the V.I.P section.

While navigating through the crowd, he is pushed from the side into someone. "Shit!" he says. He turns to see a six-foot, 200-pound black man dressed in a Burberry shirt and jeans, covered in what used to be his drink.

*Oh shit... Please don't beat me up...*

"Sorry, Man," he says.

The man just stares at him for a second. "It's cool...it's a club."

He takes a few deep breaths before continuing. "Well, at least let me get you a new drink since I made you spill yours."

"Nah, it's cool, Homie. I'm good," the man responds.

"I won't take 'no' for an answer. Let me at least get you a new drink."

The man finally accepts. "Alright."

They make their way to the bar. "What are you having?" he asks the man.

"A shot of Remy," the man replies.

He buys the shot and hands it to him. "Here you go...sorry again!"

"It's cool, Family. Thanks for the drink!"

"No problem," he responds. "Have a good one!" he says before walking off. He makes it back to the V.I.P table to find everyone there. Petey is there with his red-haired girlfriend. She has vanilla-ice-cream-colored skin and is dressed in a cocktail dress and stilettos.

"Finally!" Petey says.

"Yeah, my bad, Bro. I spilled a drink on someone, so I bought them a new one."

"Ah, well let me introduce you. This is my friend, Becky. Becky, this is my friend, JJ. He grew up with me, but now lives in Iowa."

"Nice to meet you, JJ," Becky says.

"The pleasure is all mine, Becky," he responds. He pulls up two full glasses for Petey and Becky. "Start drinking! You guys need to catch up!"

They continue to party. The crowd goes into a loud roar as the DJs switch. The bass from the huge speakers shakes the club.

"Man, these guys are pretty good!" Petey says.

"Yeah, they got some good mixes," he agrees.

The DJ comes over the loudspeaker. "Get your hands up! Get your hands up!" The lights are going crazy. Everyone is screaming. The bass is pounding faster and faster.

*Pow!*

The lights and music shut off. The club is pitch black and everyone is still screaming and cheering. A strobe light fills the club with light as the music kicks back in, and all the lights start to go wild. The crowd goes nuts.

"This is crazy!" George yells at Mindy.

"Yeah, these DJs are good! Really good!" she yells back. "Come on, George, let's dance!" She grabs his hand and pulls him towards the dance floor.

"Hey, Petey, come on!" he says.

"Where we going?" Petey asks.

"I'm going to go talk to the DJs. You with me?"

"Yeah, let's go!"

He turns to Stacy. "Hey, we will be right back."

"Where you guys going?"

"We're gonna go talk to the DJs."

"Okay...see if they'll give you their CD!"

He nods and makes his way over to the DJ booth with Petey. Ya Boy Dru Soy is spinning the beats. "Hey, what's up?" he asks the DJ.

"What's going on, guys?" Dru Soy replies.

"I just wanted to let you know, you guys play some badass music! You guys have any CDs that I would be able to buy?"

"Hold on one second, let me look." Ya Boy Dru Soy grabs a backpack and opens it. He pulls out a CD with their information on it. "Here you go," he says as he hands the CD to JJ.

"How much do we owe you?"

"Nothing, just tell all your friends about us!"

"That's why I came over. I heard you're from Iowa… What part?"

"The DMI."

"No shit? I go to school at ISU!"

"Oh yeah?" the DJ replies. "That's only like…thirty minutes from me, too."

"Do you DJ a lot back in the DMI?"

"Somewhat. I usually do parties. I'm not a resident DJ anywhere."

"I'm going to try and do a party at a club on campus. I'll get a hold of you, because I think the students would love it!"

"Yeah, get at me on the net and let me know what's good. What's your name again?"

"It's JJ."

Okay, nice to meet you, JJ!"

"Yeah, you too!"

The rest of the night is filled with more drinking and dancing. The DJ gets on the loudspeaker for last call, and they pay their bar tab.

"George, you want to come to my place?" Mindy asks.

George shoots JJ a nervous look. He smiles and nods at George. George turns and looks at Mindy. "Sure, let's go. I'll see you guys tomorrow," George says with a smile.

"Have fun, George!" he replies.

"Well, JJ, Becky wants to head home. I probably won't see you before you leave tomorrow, so drive safe and think about what we talked about earlier today."

"Okay Petey, I will. It was good to see you! Nice to meet you, Becky!"

"It was nice to meet you, too," Becky replies.

Petey looks at Stacy. "You take care of my boy JJ for me."

"Oh, I will!" Stacy replies.

Petey and Becky head down the street while JJ and Stacy walk to his car.

-----

After a full recovery from the night before, they begin to pack their clothes. George finally shows up around midday.

"Oh shit! How was last night for you?" he says, laughing.

"I think I'm in love, Bro," George replies.

"She must have turned your world upside down, huh?"

George begins to laugh. "I guess you could say that."

"Well, I'm happy for you, Bro. I'm happy you had fun, too. Get your stuff together. We need to get going soon."

They finish packing, and JJ kisses his mom and dad goodbye. The rest of them say their goodbyes and they get in the car to head back towards Iowa. As he drives, Stacy and George fall asleep. All he can think about is what Petey said about the powder. Sending it through the mail.

*Should I do it...or should I not?*

Finally, after making it back and dropping off Stacy and George, he heads back to his apartment.

He drops his bags and lies down on the couch.

Mark walks into the living room from his room. "How was your trip?"

"It was good. Did that last you...what I gave you?" he asks.

"Yeah, that's what I want to talk to you about."

The sound of Mark's tone worries him. He sits up. "What happened?"

"Well, I got half of what I owe you."

"Okay...where's the rest of it, Mark?"

"I fronted it, and the dude hasn't paid me yet."

"Okay, so when did he say he was going to pay you?"

"Well, he told me that he was going to pay me that day."

"And which day was this?"

"That was Friday night."

"Have you talked to him since then?"

"Yeah, but he just gives me the runaround."

He takes a deep breath and exhales. "You know where he lives?"

"Yeah, I do."

"Well, if you don't have it tomorrow, we're going to go collect it. Even if it means beating the dude's ass and taking his shit... We are getting paid."

"Well I..." Mark starts.

He cuts Mark off. "Well nothing, Mark. This isn't a game. This is business. People die in the drug game every day. He doesn't have cash; he pays with possessions. Plain and simple."

"Okay," Mark replies in a soft, insecure tone.

He sits back on the couch.

*I can't let this dude get away with this, because once one does, they will all try it, and I'm not going to let that happen. I need to set an example.*

# TANYA

*Ring, ring, ring.*

A familiar, young, male voice answers. "Hello?"

"Quick, what's up with the rest of that favor you owe me?" she asks.

"Damn, Family, you can't even say hello? I'm working on it, Tanya. I can't just pull the shit out of a hat, you feel me?"

"Yes, but you're taking too long. I need to take care of these loose ends."

"Okay, okay, calm down. I'll see what I can pull, okay, Cuz?"

"Alright, but remember what I said to you before...family or not."

Quick stops her mid-sentence. "No need to repeat it. I remember... Just make sure you're available."

"Okay, I will," she replies. She disconnects without another word.

*He better get this shit set up soon. I want that nigga, Teddy, dead soon.*

All she can do is think about the promise she made to her dead brother and father.

*I promise that if anyone ever messes with our family, I'll take care of them personally...and I promise to kill them up close and personal...to make sure the mistake I made that took you guys away from me will never happen again.*

As she sits and thinks about life, her phone vibrates next to her on the couch. "Who is this?" she mumbles as she reaches to pick up her phone. She looks at the call screen and sees Quick's name.

*He better be telling me something good.*

"Yes, Quick," she answers.

"Hey, make sure you come to Secrets tonight at 11:00PM... Teddy will be down there. I will introduce you to him."

"Alright, Quick, just give me a ride down there."

"Fine, Cuz, I will pick you up at your house around 10:30PM."

"Okay Quick, I'll see you then," she replies as she hangs up the phone and tosses it on the couch.

*No emotions, no feelings, Tanya...it's just a job.*

The rest the day passes and night falls. Quick arrives at the house. He steps inside without knocking. "You ready, Cuz?" he yells.

"Yeah, give me just one second," she replies. A few minutes pass before she strolls into the living room. "Okay I'm ready," she says, grabbing her phone from the table.

"Damn, Cuz, if that don't get his attention, I don't know what will," Quick replies as he begins to laugh.

"Shit, if this one piece, nearly-see-through-white-dress doesn't get him, then that little nigga is gay," she replies as she begins to laugh with him.

"Alright, let's go," Quick says.

-----

They arrive at Secrets and meet up with the group at the V.I.P tables. Teddy, a lanky guy, is standing there, as well. The dude looks to be about 120 pounds soaking wet. She begins to evaluate the area, making sure no spot goes unnoticed.

*This is a professional hit.*

Quick introduces her to Teddy. "How are you doing, Ma?" Teddy asks as he looks her up and down. She can practically see his thoughts forming on his face.

*'Damn, this bitch is bangin! With her olive-colored-skin, black hair, hazel eyes, thick lips, perky medium-sized breasts, thick ass, looking like a video girl... I'm going to fuck her tonight.'*

"I'm doing okay," she responds.

*Man, this nigga is staring hard... This shit's too easy.*

The night goes as planned. She parties with his group, taking shots but spitting them back into a half-empty beer bottle. She only wants him to *think* she's getting wasted.

Quick stops by. "Hey, you guys want some ecstasy?"

Teddy looks at him and nods. "Yeah, give me two."

Quick pulls out two clear gel-caps and hands them to Teddy. "I need $40 for the pills."

Teddy pulls out two $20 bills and hands them to Quick, then turns to her and sticks out his hand.

"Here...take this with me."

"Okay," she replies as she takes the gel-cap from him, but before she takes hers, she waits for him to drink his down first. After he does, she picks up the bottle she has been spitting in all night and acts like she drinks it down. The pill falls from her mouth into the bottle. "Ahh," she says like a true actress.

"Thanks, Teddy."

Teddy smiles. "No problem."

After an hour or so, she notices Teddy is peaking. "Come on, let's dance Teddy," she says as she grabs his hand and takes him onto the dance floor.

They begin dancing, grinding on each other. She grabs his hands and places them on her breasts. He begins rubbing her all over and kissing her neck. She lets off a soft moan, then turns around to face him. She grabs his cock through his pants and bites her lower lip. "Damn, Daddy, this ecstasy got me horny as fuck," she whispers in his ear.

"So, what's good? You want to go to my place?" Teddy asks.

"Yeah, let's go. Can you drive?"

"Yes, I'm good, Ma. Let's go."

-----

A block away, Smurf pulls up to a red light. He's almost done making his rounds. Just one more stop on the east side, and he can call it a night. He's still waiting for the light to change, when he notices a black Impala stop across the intersection. He recognizes the driver instantly. It's one of the guys that jumped him in jail. Tanya is in the passenger seat.

*What the fuck is she doing with him? I'm done with this shit. I'm going to kill him, then her!*

-----

They arrive at a ranch-style home on the lower south side. "This it?" she asks.

"Yep," he replies as he gets out of the car. As they make their way to the front door, she reaches in her purse and feels her gun, just waiting to claim another lost soul. She has no idea Smurf is watching her every move from a few houses down.

After entering the house, Teddy grabs her by the hand and leads her to the bedroom. "Nice place," she says.

"Thanks," he replies as he flips on the lights.

He pushes her onto the bed and begins trying to kiss her, but she stops him. "Nope," she says softly. He looks at her, confused. "What? I'm not your girlfriend. We are just fucking... You can kiss anything but my lips. Save that for your girl." She pushes him off and onto the other side of the bed.

"Let me take care of you, Daddy."

She pulls up his shirt and begins kissing his stomach, working her way up to his neck. She begins to suck on it softly. "How's that feel?" she moans into his ear.

"Good...real good," he replies. His speech is slurred from the ecstasy. She pulls his shirt off, revealing his scrawny, tattooed body and continues to let her hands run wild. She slowly unbuttons and unzips his pants.

"I've never done this on ecstasy before," she moans as she tugs his pants and boxers off. "You having fun yet?" she moans as she begins to lick the head of his cock.

"Yeah," he moans. She continues to lick the tip. Her tongue moves slowly down the shaft to his balls and back up to the head.

"How does that feel?" she says, while tapping the head of his cock on her perked up lips.

"Shit...good, Ma...keep going," he moans. She slowly starts to swallow his partially-hard cock, inching it in until he is balls deep in her mouth. "Fuck!" he moans as she continues to bob her head up and down.

"Hmmm, I'm getting wet," she moans as she starts jerking him off.

"Get up here," he says as he pulls her up onto the bed. He pushes her onto her back.

"Eat my pussy," she moans. She helps him lift her dress up.

"Damn, Ma, this pussy is juicy," he moans as he slowly opens her lips, revealing her swollen clit.

He begins licking it with the tip of his tongue.

"Right there, ohh," she moans as she pushes his head deep into her pussy.

*This dude has a great head game!*

She rubs her fingers through his hair. "You have a condom, right?" she moans.

"Yeah," he responds as he gets up and grabs a condom from his nightstand.

*I hope his sex game is as good as his head game.*

He rips open the package and rolls it over his cock. He slowly slides inside her, inch by inch, until he is fully in.

"Hmm," she moans as she arches her back and takes the fullness inside of her. He starts pumping hard.

*It's too bad he's going to die tonight.*

He continues to pump her. "Harder, harder," she moans. A sound comes from the hallway.

"What was that?" she asks, stopping him.

"What was what, Ma?" he replies.

"I heard something."

"Don't worry, it was nothing. Trust me, Ma. Don't worry about it."

"I want to get on top," she moans. He pulls out and lies on his back. She straddles him and holds up his cock, slowly lowering herself onto it. "Oh God," she moans as she starts riding up and down.

"Fuck, I'm going to come," he grunts

"No, not yet...me first," she moans as she starts riding faster. She begins to feel the sensations. It starts in her toes and works its way up, inching up into her pussy. "I can't take it, I'm coming!" she screams as her body starts to shake.

He continues bouncing her up and down. "Fuck, I'm about to come," he moans. She can feel the pulsating of his cock releasing his load all over the condom inside her.

"Hmmm, how was that?" she moans. The ecstasy has him so messed up, he can't even talk. "I need to get cleaned up," she says. She gets off him and retrieves her purse.

She goes into the attached bathroom and closes the door. She looks at herself in the mirror, but all she can see is her family, Jeff and her life.

*Get yourself together. You're here to do a job.*

She pulls the gun from her purse and clicks off the safety. "You okay in there?" he yells.

"Yes, I'm just using the bathroom," she replies as she connects the silencer and puts it back in her purse.

*Just finish the job.*

She holds the gun behind her back and steps back into the bedroom. She stops midstride as she stares at Teddy, who is holding a chrome-plated gun. It's aimed right at her.

"You didn't think I was going to let you pull that 'okie-dokie' shit on me, did you?" he says.

She can feel the blood leave her face.

*Is this it?*

She stares at him and the gun.

"You're a pretty slick bitch, but not slick enough. I was at the club the night you left with Leo, so I know it was you that killed him." All she can do is stare at him. "But I must ask, what made you want to do this?" Teddy asks.

"You killed my boyfriend, Nigga!" she yells.

"Oh, Jeff was your boyfriend? That's too bad, but it's okay, ma. You and that nigga, Smurf, will be seeing him very soon," he replies as he clicks the hammer on the gun back.

*Pow, pow!*

Shots ring off from the hallway. She ducks into the bathroom and watches as Teddy, hit by one of the shots, jumps through the bedroom window. She pulls up her gun and returns fire through the wall in the bathroom.

*Pow, pow, pow!*

A barrage of shots ring back-and-forth, echoing throughout the house. She is almost out of ammunition. She lets off one last shot.

*Pow!*

The house goes quiet. She slowly gets up and peeks her gun around the wall, followed by her head. She is now staring down the barrel of a black, 9mm handgun. Smurf is standing at the end of it.

# JJ

JJ awakens with a stretch and a sigh. He has a full schedule ahead of him.

*I need to get an apartment to set this lab up, and I still need to pay George his cut...if Mark ever gets paid...and if that doesn't happen, I need to take care of that problem, too.*

He rolls out of bed and gets on the computer to search for apartments. He's choosing his search carefully, trying to find a place that will allow him to pay with cash without asking for his name. After searching for about twenty minutes, he finds an apartment that might just work. The Cyclone Apartments are located on the west side of town. It's a bit out of the way, which is good. It's only $400 a month for a one bedroom, and they don't do any background checks.

*I'll check this out today.*

He gets dressed and grabs $3,000 in cash and stashes it in his pocket. He leaves the apartment and drives to the west side of town to follow up on the apartment. He pulls up to the office and parks his car.

Inside, a young man is sitting at a decently-sized desk. He is in his early twenties and has short, black hair. The man looks up from his papers when he hears the office door open. "Hello, how can I help you?"

"I'm looking to rent an apartment here. One bedroom if possible," he replies.

"We have a few one bedrooms available."

"Okay, good."

"Let me grab a key." The guy grabs a large key ring from a hook on the wall. They leave the main office and walk towards the apartment. "Can I ask you question?"

"What's up?" he replies.

"You look familiar... Do you attend ISU?"

"Yes, I do. Do you?"

"Yeah, I'm an accounting major."

"Oh really?" he replies. "That's good. Everybody needs an accountant."

"What about you? What's your major?" the young man asks.

"Mine's chemical engineering."

"Oh, an engineer! I heard that's a hard field of study."

He laughs. "It's alright. For me, school is pretty easy, so I don't complain." He pauses. "I'm sorry, I didn't introduce myself. I'm JJ, what is your name?"

"My name's Chris Fleming."

"Nice to meet you, Chris."

"Yeah, you too, JJ. Let's check this apartment out."

As they walk around the inside of the apartment, he assesses the potential.

*This is okay... It's a decent spot, not too big and not too small. This would definitely work for the lab.*

"Hey, Chris, can I ask you a question?"

"Sure, what is it?"

"You make a lot of money working here?"

Chris laughs. "Well, I wouldn't say I could become a millionaire working for these people, but it does pay the bills."

"What is it you get paid per hour? Or salary?"

Chris hesitates before answering. "I get paid $8 an hour."

"I see; I see," he replies as he rests his hand on the left side of his face.

"So JJ, what do you think of the apartment?"

"I like it, and I'll take it, but I got a problem."

"What's that?"

"I have bad credit, so is there any way I could get it in someone else's name?"

Chris gives JJ a weird look, trying to see through his words. "I'm not supposed to do that."

"Well, Chris, everything has a price. How much will it cost for you to do it?"

Chris thinks for a few minutes. "I'll do it for $300," he says in a nervous voice.

He nods his head. "Alright, Chris, I got you." He pulls out three $100 bills from his pocket and places them in Chris' hand. "So, we good?"

"Yeah, JJ, we are good. Come with me back to the office, and we will get this stuff filled out."

He follows Chris back the office and sits down in the chair across the desk. "Okay, JJ, it's going to be $400 a month, and I need first and last months' rent today. Rent is due the third of every month."

"Okay, Chris, I'll tell you what... You seem like a pretty cool guy, and since you're helping me out, I'm willing to help you out. I'll give you

$1,000 right now...$800 for the apartment, and the other $200 is yours. Plus, I will give you $500 a month. $400 of that goes to the apartment, and the other $100 is yours...and I will do this every month. How does that sound?"

Chris just stares at JJ from across the desk. "You're seriously going to do that for me?"

"Yeah! You helped me out, so I'll help you out. The one thing I ask is that you keep this between me and you only, please."

"No problem, JJ. This stays between you and me only," Chris repeats.

"Okay, good, that's what I wanted to hear." He pulls out $1,000 in $100s and hands it to Chris.

"This covers what I owe you. Can I get that key now?"

"Yeah, here you go," Chris replies as he drops the key into his hand. "Your apartment number is the one we looked at...number eighteen."

"Okay, great! So, Chris, you're going to go ahead and take care of the paper work?"

"Yeah, I got that covered. You're good to go, JJ!"

"Okay great." They shake hands, and he walks towards the door. He turns around again before leaving. "One more time...thanks again,

Chris. I appreciate it!"

Chris smiles and says, "Not a problem."

He gets in his car and checks his funds.

*Well shit, I'm out. I might as well run around and collect.*

He stops at Leon's first and picks up the $8,400 that was owed to him. Now he has enough to pay George his half of $5,100. He pulls out his cell and calls George.

"Hello?"

"Hey, George, what are you doing?"

"Hey, JJ, I'm at the shooting range. What's up?"

"You're at the shooting range? Where is that?"

"It's just north of town, why? You want to come up here?"

"Yeah, I need to see you real quick. How do I get there?"

"Take the highway through town and follow it north for about ten miles. You will see the sign on the left; it's called Hawkeye Shooting Range."

"Okay, I'll be there in probably twenty minutes."

"Okay, I'll see you soon," George responds.

*I never knew George was into that type of stuff... I guess there is a lot I don't know about him.*

He arrives at the range and parks his car off to the side. He counts out $5,100 and puts it in his pocket. He places the rest of his money into the center console and gets out to find George.

He spots George at the end by himself. The loud pops from George's gun make his ears ring.

"George!" he yells.

George slowly turns toward JJ. "Oh hey, JJ," he says as he puts the handgun down and lowers his ear protectors. "You found it!"

"Yeah, George, you're pretty good with directions."

"So, what's up, JJ? Did you need to see me?"

"Yeah. I wanted to talk to you."

"Alright, what's going on?"

"First, I got your cut from this last batch."

"When do I need to pick it up?" George asks.

"You don't. I have the money on me," he replies as he pulls the rolled up money out of his pocket. He hands it to George. "Second, I got an apartment west of town at the Cyclone Apartments for our set up, but we need to get someone to put the electricity and water in their name."

"We can just do it in mine," George responds.

He is hesitant about this. "I don't know."

"Why not, JJ? Only you and Mark know I'm involved in this, so we will just do it in my name. You got a pen? If so, write down the address and the apartment number, and I'll do it tomorrow."

"Yeah, I think I got a pen in my car. I will write it down before I leave. He pauses and listens to the silence. His eyes focus back on George's gun. "George, I didn't know you were into guns and that stuff."

"Yeah, I've been hunting with my dad since I was little. You ever shot before?"

"No, I have not."

"Come on, I will show you how to shoot... You never know, it might one day save your life or the life of someone you love."

"Okay, I'll try it."

"Okay first, you need to stand with your feet shoulder-width apart. Either left foot in front of right or vice versa, whichever is comfortable for you."

"Okay, I like it this way," he responds after finding his position.

"Okay, next, put your right arm out with a slight bend at the elbow." He obeys. "Now put the gun in your right hand. Don't be scared to hold it. The safety is on."

He puts the gun in his right hand as instructed. "Okay, what next George?"

"Now grip the other half of the gun handle tightly with a slight bend in the elbow for the gun's recoil." George waits for him to get into position before continuing again. "Now aim down the site on the top of the gun, toward your target."

He cocks his head, closes one eye and looks down the top of the gun. "Now what?"

"I'm going to support you for your first time until you get the feel for the recoil."

"Okay."

George wraps around him and supports his arms. "Are you ready, JJ?"

"Yeah," he replies.

"Okay," George responds as he clicks off the safety. "Ready...fire!" He pulls the trigger. The explosion and the echo from the gun shocks him.

He turns and looks at George. "Holy shit!" He laughs.

"What do you think, JJ?"

"That was fun! Can we do it again?"

"Sure, go ahead! Aim the gun; do everything like I told you... You ready?"

"Yep," he responds. He pulls the trigger again. After the recoil, he laughs. "George, this is cool!"

"Well, JJ, I'm happy you like it. I'll teach you how to be an ace shot!"

"Sweet! Sounds good, George!" He looks down at the time on his cell phone. "Damn...I gotta go, George. I'll just write down the address for you."

"Okay, cool. I'll do that stuff tomorrow, JJ."

"Alright, sounds good." He returns to his car and writes down the address. He comes back and hands it to George. "Here you go. Here is the address."

"Alright, thanks, JJ. I will do it tomorrow."

"That's fine. Thanks again for the shooting lesson!"

"Yeah, no problem! I'll see you later." George turns back to his station, and he walks back to his car.

He leaves the gun range and heads back to his apartment. Mark isn't there when he arrives, but he can wait. He starts boxing up all the lab glassware, getting it ready for the move.

*No one other than George and I can know about this.*

Mark shows up after two hours. "Hey, Mark, what's the word on that dude?" Mark shakes his head. "Okay, fuck it. Let's go to this guy's house and collect our money." Mark says nothing, but follows him out to his car.

They get in his car, and Mark gives him directions. They arrive at a two-story, white house with red shutters and a red door.

"You ready, Mark? You're doing the talking."

"Yeah, I guess."

"Well, first things first, Mark... No mentioning of my name, because if this dude doesn't have our money, we're beating his ass."

"Come on, JJ, we don't need to beat him up, Man."

"Mark, this is the first snag in our business chain. If we let this dude get away with this, everyone will try and test us, so we need to set an example, so no one will fuck with us...at least not you."

Mark exhales loudly. "You're the boss, JJ."

*I'm the boss... That's nice to hear.*

"Let's do this," Mark says as he gets out of the car and heads to the front door. Mark knocks repeatedly until a man answers. The guy looks like an old hippie. He's an older guy with long, brown hair and a mustache. They enter the house.

Once in the living room, Mark and the man begin talking. "Hey, where is your bathroom?" JJ asks.

The man looks at him. "It's down the hall and on the right."

"Thanks," he says. He walks down the hall and goes into the kitchen. He doesn't need to use the bathroom. He starts searching for a weapon and finds a medium-sized skillet.

*This will work.*

He leaves the kitchen and heads back to the living room. As he gets closer, he hears Mark and the man arguing. "I need that money!" Mark yells.

"Well, I don't have it!"

"Then where is it?"

"I spent it, Man!" the man says.

"I owe that money," Mark replies.

"Well, I don't know what to tell you, Mark."

"Give me something to cover the cost then," Mark replies.

*I've heard enough.*

He enters the living room and catches the man with his back facing him. He hits him over the head with the skillet and doesn't stop.

"No!" Mark yells as he watches JJ beat the unconscious man.

"Motherfucker!" he yells at the man. "He told you he needs his money!" He kicks the man a few more times and turns to Mark. "Does anyone else owe?"

Mark begins to stutter. "No...no...no one else."

"Alright, fine. Mark, I need you to search the house for money, drugs...anything worth monetary value... you grab. You understand me? Anything worth money, you take it. I'll teach this bitch a lesson." He turns back to the man on the ground. "Don't fuck with us!" he yells. He calls out to Mark again.

"And don't forget, you owe me $840, Mark, so I better get paid!"

After about thirty minutes of ransacking the house, Mark returns. "I got it."

"What did you find?" he asks.

"I found his stash spot."

"What did he have?"

"He had the money owed for the ounces of hydroponic marijuana and the molly we sold him."

"You grabbed it all, right?" he asks.

"Yeah, I did. Come on, let's go!" Mark yells.

"Alright, but we leave the house acting normal... We don't need to draw any attention."

"Okay."

"Come on, let's go." They leave and walk to the car as if nothing happened. They make it back to the apartment where they divvy up the money.

"Mark?"

"Yeah, JJ?"

"Just give me the $840 you owe me and keep the rest."

"Seriously?"

"Yeah, but a word to the wise: Sell what you have and get paid. Slow down on getting high all the time and change your number. Never fuck with that bitch-ass dude again, alright?"

"Yeah, JJ. I'm not messing with him anymore. I just wish we didn't have to beat him."

"Well, Mark, this is a dog-eat-dog world, and it's not for the weak-hearted. Sometimes people need to be taught a lesson. So, you teach it to them. If it's a beat down, so be it. But one thing is certain… No one gets over on us, because once they do, we're in trouble. Everyone will think we're soft, and we can't have that."

"Where did you learn all this at?" Mark asks.

He just looks at Mark and starts laughing. He sits on the couch. "Don't you ever watch movies?"

# SMURF

"Where are we going?" Tanya asks as tears run down her face.

"My house. We need to talk about some things," he replies. They pull in his driveway and go inside. "You want to smoke?" he asks.

"Yeah, please... I need a hit after all this shit."

"I'll right back," he says. He goes into the next room and returns with a plastic baggie filled with blueberry-smelling marijuana and blunt wraps. "Here, roll this," he says as he tosses the stuff onto the table. He goes into another room to find a lighter.

When he returns again, he stops midway into the room. A cold chill runs up his spine as he sees Tanya sitting with a gun aimed at him.

*Shit...this bitch.*

"Don't even reach for your piece, or I'll put two in your chest," she says with no emotion.

*Who is this bitch?... this cold-hearted, killing bitch?...*

He slowly raises his hands away from his waist. "Now I got some questions for you," she says.

He glares at her. "What is it?"

"First, how did you know where I was?"

"I saw that you caught a ride with that punk bitch in his car, so I followed you to his house."

"How long were you there?"

"Long enough to know you fucked that nigga!" he yells.

She just sits there silently, again with no emotion. "What the fuck are you and Jeff caught up in with that nigga, Junior? Why do they want you dead so badly, Smurf?"

"You know I went to jail for a triple murder?"

"Yeah, I know...what about it?"

"Well, it was for the deaths of Old man Smoke, his wife, and some other punk-ass nigga."

"Old Man Smoke?" she asks.

"Yeah, well his son, Smoke Jr., and some of his little buddies decided to jump on me one night while I was in jail with Jeff, and we got into a fight with Teddy and Leo over the incident and ended up whooping them little niggas asses real bad."

"...it's all starting to make sense," she replies.

"But I think the hit was meant for me. I really don't think they knew it was Jeff, and for that, I'm sorry," he replies. She says nothing as she begins to cry. "But enough about me, now answer some of my questions… What the fuck were you doing with him?" he yells.

"I was getting him back for what he did to Jeff. I wanted him dead, Smurf! If Jeff can't live, neither can he!"

*How can a girl like her look so innocent, and yet, be so damn deadly?*

"What's your story?" he asks.

"What do you mean *my story*?" she replies.

"Well, what about your family…and where did you learn how to shoot like Lara Croft?"

"Well, my mother moved to Florida after my brother and father were killed in a car crash, so I lived by myself for a while, until I had my little cousin move up here with me. Her boyfriend at the time taught me how to shoot."

"Shit, I need to meet him," he says as he begins to laugh. "Can I sit down now?" he asks.

"Yes, come on," she responds as she puts the gun on the table.

He slowly makes his way to the couch and sits down next her. "Do you still want to smoke?" he asks.

"Yeah, I'll roll it." She cleans the weed and rolls the blunt. After finishing, she lights it up and takes two big hits. She passes it to him, and he takes a few hits. All he can think about is the barrage of recent insanity. The death of his right-hand-man Jeff, and just life in general.

They continue to smoke as they watch TV. She takes another hit and slowly lowers her head and leans against his shoulder. At first he stays completely still, but then repositions his arm around her and pulls her closer. She slowly wraps her arm around his waist and takes a long and relaxing deep breath before closing her eyes.

-----

She awakens the next morning and finds herself still on the couch, but wrapped in a blanket. She lets off a soft moan as she stretches her arms. The smell of food fills her lungs with each deep breath.

She gets up and follows the smell to the kitchen where Smurf is cooking breakfast.

"You're finally up I see," he says as she walks in.

"Yeah, I'm up... What are you cooking? It smells great."

"Just making some breakfast...some eggs and French toast. I figured you would be hungry," he replies.

"Ah, thanks, Smurf," she replies in an unusually girly voice.

"Go ahead and get something to drink and sit at the table. I'll be done in a few minutes."

She sits and checks her phone. He makes two plates and sets one in front of her and they begin eating.

"Damn, this is good! Where did you learn to cook?"

"My mother. I helped her cook a lot," he replies. She washes the food down with a glass of orange juice, then continues to eat. "Hey, Tanya..."

"What's up?" she replies, taking another drink.

"We made the news today."

She stops short and starts coughing. "What? What do you mean we made the news?"

"This morning...they were talking about a shooting at a house, and it just happened to be Teddy's house."

"Shit..." she responds.

"Don't worry. They don't have any leads, so I doubt much will come from it."

"I hope not," she responds, still visibly nervous. Her phone begins to ring, and she gets up quickly to answer it in the living room. He leans a bit in her direction and hears her half of the conversation.

"Hello?... No, I am free... I'm not busy...You want me to meet you? ...Okay, I'll be there in an hour."

He watches her close her phone and head back towards the kitchen. "I'm sorry, Smurf, but we have to cut this short... Can you give me a ride to my cousin's house?"

"Yeah, but can we finish eating first? Then I'll take you to your family's house?" She nods.

They finish eating and leave. "Where does your cousin live?" he asks, starting the truck.

"She lives downtown by Michigan Avenue."

"Oh yeah? Your family has some money, huh?"

She pauses before answering. "Well, my family from Miami does."

He nods and keeps driving. They finally stop in front of a large skyscraper, no doubt filled with condominiums.

"Thanks again. I'll talk you later," she says as she exits the car.

"Yes, see you later," he replies as she closes the door. He watches her walk to the main entrance, her sexy ass swaying back and forth. He shakes his head and refocuses.

*Shit...I might as well pick up some cash at some of my spots.*

He puts the car in drive and heads down the road to make his rounds.

-----

A few hours later, he is back at his place with a wad of money. He sits down on the couch and begins organizing the money on the coffee table. His money machine sits at the end of the table. He runs each pile through the machine and rubber bands it. He makes a few stacks before picking up his phone.

He scrolls to Papi's number and calls.

"Hello?"

"Papi, are you available?" he asks.

"I'm actually getting ready. I'm going out of town this weekend.

"Well can I pick up four videos from you...to watch over the weekend?"

"Sure," Papi responds. "Come by in an hour or so. I should be done packing by then."

"Okay, I'll call you back," he replies, then hangs up. He now has time to kill. He decides to smoke a blunt. Within minutes he is inhaling and exhaling large clouds of smoke. He closes his eyes and relaxes as the THC works through his system.

He awakens nearly three hours later and immediately checks his watch.

*Shit!*

He frantically reaches for his phone to call Papi. He finds his number and calls. It rings for a long time, but no answer. He ends the call and scrolls through his contacts until he gets to Tanya's number.

"Hello?" she answers.

"Hey, Tanya, what's up?"

"Nothing too much. What's up?"

"Nothing. Hey, have you talked to Papi?"

"Yeah, a couple hours ago...why?"

"Well I was supposed to get some movies from him, but he won't answer now."

"How many?"

"Four."

"Okay, let me call him, and I'll call you back."

"Alright," he says and disconnects.

Tanya finally calls back after a few hours. "Hello," he answers.

"Hey, I talked to Papi, and he dropped those movies off to me, so come get them."

"Okay. Are you at the place I dropped you off at earlier?"

"Yes, I'm still here."

"Okay, I'll be down there in thirty minutes."

"Okay, and don't forget to bring the loot."

"I won't." He ends the call and leaves his place.

He arrives at the condo downtown and calls her. "Hey, what level do you live on?"

"Level ten, room number 103. It will be unlocked."

"Okay, see you in a second." He walks in the main entrance and finds the elevators. When he arrives at her door, he knocks twice before entering.

*Damn, this place is nice!*

He waits a few seconds before letting himself in. "Hello?" he yells.

A voice yells back, telling him to come to living room. He follows a long, fancy hallway down to a large living room filled with very expensive furniture and accessories.

"Hey, Smurf. Come in, come in. Sit down," Tanya says as she pats the spot on the couch next to her.

"This is nice," he replies as he takes a seat on the suede couch.

She shrugs. "It's alright."

"So, did he get you those four movies I needed?"

"Yep." She gets up and leaves the room and returns with four sealed kilos of powder cocaine.

"Here you go. Did you bring the money? How much did he charge you?"

"Yeah, I got the money. I've been getting them for eighteen each."

"Oh, he told me that since you been doing really good it's going down to sixteen each now."

"Seriously?" he responds.

"Yeah...I almost forgot to tell you that."

"Shit, I'm not going to complain!" He pulls out the money and begins to count it. "So I owe you sixty-four, right?"

"Yes, $64,000." He starts making stacks, and she picks up some bills and does the same. Smurf is beginning to notice a lot about Tanya.

*Man, this girl counts money like a pro, shoots like a pro and has a killer mentality. What's up with this girl?* They continue to count. "The first sixteen I owe you," he says as he hands it to her and watches her set the finished stack of cash next to her feet.

Finally, after half an hour or so of counting, she has six $10,000 stacks next to her and one $4,000 stack. She looks down at the money, and then looks up at him. "Looks like we're good." She piles the stacks together and takes them into another room.

He grabs the remaining money sitting on the table and puts it back into his pockets. He moves the kilos of cocaine over to his side of the couch and sits back in his spot.

She returns. "Are you thirsty?"

"Yeah, I will take something to drink," he replies.

"Come on, follow me to the kitchen," she says as she motions with her arm.

The kitchen is even nicer than the last room. It's filled with stainless steel appliances and maple cabinets. Marble countertops frame the room, and in the center of the kitchen is an island with a stove and a metal vent hanging above it.

"This is a dope kitchen! This shit looks like it cost a pretty penny!"

She turns and smiles as she opens up the refrigerator. "What do you want?"

"A cold soda if you got one," he replies.

"I have cold Pepsi...is that okay?"

"Yeah, that's fine," he responds as he takes the soda from her.

"Come on, I'll show you around the place." She takes him from room to room, giving a general tour. Each room seems just as elegant as the last.

*This family truly does have a lot of money.*

They return to the living room, and he stares out the window. "This is a dope spot, especially with this view."

She smiles and looks out the window, next to him. "I definitely love the view from this place."

She turns her gaze from the city to him. "What are you doing tonight?"

"I don't know…nothing. Probably just chill. Why, what's going on?"

"Well, my cousin is having a party tonight. I guess her boyfriend and one of his friends are in town. I was going to say, if you're not doing anything, you should stop by and hang out tonight."

"Yeah, it sounds cool with me. What time do you want me to come back?"

"I'll have my cousin drop me off at your house, and we'll smoke there and come together."

"Why don't I just meet you here?"

"I want to give my cousin and her man some time to chill, you know what I mean?"

"Yeah, I feel you. If you want to come kick it at my place for a while to give them some alone time, that's cool with me."

"Okay, well, it's 6:30 now... Is it cool if I show up around 10:30?"

"Yeah, I need to stop at some places, then I'll be back at my place to shower and get ready."

"Okay, Smurf. So I will see you at your place at 10:30 tonight."

"Yeah. I better get going. I still need to stop at those places before you come over tonight," he says as he stands up.

"Hold on one second, Smurf. Let me get you a bag for that stuff." She leaves the room and comes back with a simple, black bag.

He places the kilos into the bag and throws it over his shoulder. "I'll see you soon," he says before leaving. He makes all of his intended stops, dropping off the packages he just got from Tanya.

This will keep his people busy for the night.

After returning home, he hops in the shower. He changes into a nice set of Sean John jeans and a Gucci, button-down, dress shirt. While in the bathroom, he hears a knock at the door. "It's unlocked!" he yells.

He hears the door open, followed by the clicking of high heels walking towards the kitchen.

"Where you at?" Tanya yells.

"I'm in the bathroom!"

"Okay, I'll wait for you out here."

He finishes getting ready and comes out to find her sitting on the couch, rolling a blunt.

*Damn, I don't even have to ask her to roll one now.*

He begins to laugh. She looks up and smiles. "I was bored waiting for your slow ass, and I saw the weed and the blunt wraps. We'll smoke this, and then we can go to the party."

He walks over and sits down on the couch. She finishes rolling the blunt and looks at him. "Look at you, Smurf. Who are you trying to impress?"

He just shakes his head. "Well, look at you, all dressed up in a tight shirt and a miniskirt... Who are *you* trying to pick up?"

She smiles. "Touché, touché...but enough about that. Come on, let's smoke this and get going," she says as she lights up and passes the blunt to him. They continue to smoke until 11:30PM.

"Are you ready to go?" he asks her.

"Yeah, let's get going," she replies.

They hop into his SUV and make their way towards downtown. "Let's get some liquor for this thing," he says. She nods in agreement.

They stop by the local liquor store down the street from his house. He runs in and returns with a bottle of Remington. "I think this should last," he says as he passes the case off to her.

"Yeah, this will last all night," she replies.

They finally get downtown, find a spot to park and make their way inside the building. While riding the elevator, he looks at Tanya. He licks his lips slightly, like an animal waiting for a meal. He remembers the first time he met her.

They exit and walk down to a door. She pulls out a key and opens the door. Inside, there are beautiful people of all types and ethnicities running around.

*Now, this is going to be a party.*

# JJ *several months later*

"Hello?" he answers, still a bit groggy.

"Come on, JJ, it's the afternoon! Why are you still sleeping? Long night last night?" The voice begins to laugh.

He moans. "I guess you could say that. What's up, Petey? What do you need?"

"Well, I called to let you know that you should be getting a present from me today."

"Okay, good. I was wondering when I was going to get it."

"I know, I know. I had some issues come up, so it took me longer than usual."

"Everything straight? Because all it takes is one kink in the chain to stop the bike from moving."

"Yes, everything is good. Just call me when it gets there, alright?"

"Okay, I will hit you up later today."

"Alright, Fool. Go back to sleep," Petey says, laughing again. He hangs up and continues to lay in bed. He's still tired from the night before, but all he can do is think about his third failed attempt with George at the creation of their super drug.

*Man, we're missing something... but what are we missing?*

The thought repeats itself as he thinks about his test subject, Mark, taking dose after dose with no effect. He pulls out his phone and dials George's number.

"Hello?" George answers.

"Hey, Bro, were you sleeping?" he asks.

"Sorta. I'm stuck between awake and asleep, but what's going on, JJ?"

"Man, this third attempt keeps fucking with my head. We're missing something; I know it."

"JJ, we've been at it heavy the last few months with no luck... Maybe we should take a break and do more research."

"No...we're on the right track... I just think we're forgetting one or two steps. When can you meet me at the spot?"

"Man," George says in a reluctant voice. "I guess 4:00. I need to get some more sleep, or it's just going to be a waste of time."

"Okay, get to bed. I need your brain on its A-game. I feel it today."

"Okay, JJ. I'll meet you there at 4:00," George says.

"Okay, Bro. Get some sleep. I'll see you in a few," he replies, then closes his phone. The next few hours go by pretty slow as he gets ready for the day. He showers and changes clothes, then packs up his laptop. He warms up some leftover pizza and sits on the couch. While eating, he receives a text from Amy, Mark's girlfriend.

Hey it's here.

He heads back to his room to the safe in his closet and presses the number code into the keypad. He opens the safe, revealing at least $100,000 in large bills. He reaches into the stack of $20 bills and removes $400 from the stack. He places them into his hidden pocket on his hoodie, then closes the safe and heads back to the living room.

After finishing his pizza, he grabs his backpack and car keys and leaves his apartment. He's going to meet Amy at the post office so he can pick up his package from Petey.

He thinks about is how the business has blown up over the last eight months, just from selling at the school to all the major colleges in Iowa through the Lambda Lambda Lambda frat brothers. He gets major cities like Chicago, through Petey, and Minneapolis, through Mindy's little brother, Alex. He even has connections through his cousin Leon.

*We're getting too big, too fast. We need this super drug to work, because we'll have twelve to eighteen months to unload it before it's outlawed. Man, it's good that Amy got that job at the post office for me. I would still be selling just at the school.*

He pulls up to the post office and heads to the front counter. "Hey, JJ," Amy says with a smile.

"Amy, thanks for getting ahold of me."

"Yeah, no problem." She reaches under the desk and pulls out an 8.5 x 11 x 6 inch box and hands it to him. "Here you go."

"Thanks" he replies. "I'll put it in your car."

"Yeah that's fine," she responds.

"Thanks again!" he replies before leaving the building. He walks over to a small compact car and pulls out the $400 in cash. He places it into her glove box, then heads back to his car.

He drives to a local park and parks his car. He opens up the box and begins pulling out large piles of money. He begins counting and puts some in his pockets. He still has to meet George soon.

While heading out to the spot, he stops by a local grocery store and tosses the cardboard box into the trash. Once at the spot, he pulls out his key and enters the tiny apartment. He starts pulling the money out and placing it on the table in front of him.

JJ is still sorting the money when George enters the apartment. "Hey, JJ. Oh, did we get a package today?"

"Yeah, we got it."

"Did he collect that stuff from Alex?" George asks.

"Yeah, he did. What did Alex owe for?" JJ asks.

"I think it was ten ounces," George replies.

"Well, we will count the money, because Petey owes for eight, so we should have money for eighteen ounces of molecule powder."

"Okay," George says as he sits down. "What type of money stacks are we doing?" George asks.

"Put them in $5,000 stacks. We should have $18,000 total," he tells George. They begin counting the money and end up with three $5,000 stacks and one $3000.

"Well, it's all here, so he must of got that money from Alex," he says as he turns to George. He pushes one of the $5,000 stacks to George, and then pulls one over for himself. He pulls $1,000 from the last $5,000 stack and places it with the $3,000 stack and pushes it to George.

"There's your cut, and here is my cut. You get paid $9,000. I get paid $9,000. It's a 50-50 split." George takes the money and shoves it into his pockets. "That's cool," he says.

JJ places his money into his backpack, then he pulls out his laptop and sets it on the table. "So JJ, where do you think we're missing that extra step?" George asks as he sits on the couch facing towards JJ's computer.

"I'm not quite sure," he says as he types in his password. He starts to maneuver through several different screens until he finally reaches a hidden file that's filled with all of their research. They begin racking their brains and going back over notes from previous experiments.

"What's the hurry with this anyways? If you don't mind me asking," George says.

"Well, George, I did research on state and federal laws for this drug we're selling. I figured that it takes the government anywhere from twelve to eighteen months to outlaw a drug. So if we get it out soon, we got twelve months for sure to unload it to the world. If this drug we're creating is anything like I think it will be, this will run all other drug dealers out of business. All we do is hook up with big partnerships to push it, and we'll just wholesale to them."

"Well, JJ, maybe we should take on a lawyer to make sure we got a legal backing. I have a friend who has a cousin that is a state and federal criminal defense lawyer," George replies.

"Okay. Ask him and find out how much his services will cost, and we'll go from there," he responds. George nods, and they continue to search through the notes, trying to figure out where they keep messing up.

As George looks through the formula, he notices there's something different at the fifth step. "Hey, JJ...here on step five and step six, do you think if we add a natural chemical from plant we can extract its properties, then reintroduce it into the formula between steps five and six?" George shows JJ a picture of a plant on the laptop.

"It might just work, but where can we find that George?"

George looks at JJ and smiles. "Actually, we can find it any local plant store."

"Really? It's that easy?"

"Yes! It's actually a very common plant. While I'll run to the store, you want to set up the lab to do a chemical extraction?" George asks.

"Yes, that's fine. You do that and I'll set up the lab."

George gets up and leaves the apartment. As soon as George

leaves, JJ heads into the bedroom to set up the lab for the extraction.
He finishes the set up and goes back out to the couch to hang out. He
pulls out his phone and texts Petey.

Hey we're good dude. Thank you.

He presses SEND and continues to search on his computer for other
options, in case this natural herb doesn't work.

After a while, George comes back with five plants. "Why did you
get five plants, George?" he asks.

"Just in case we need more. Better to have too much than too
little."

"Ain't that the truth! Come on, let's do this."

They begin the extraction process. It's slow going, but after a few
hours, they have their liquid solution. Now they can begin the actual
experiment. They add the liquid in, between steps five and six.

"This process isn't going to take as long as the MDMA, because
there are fewer chemicals we have to extract," George tells him.

They continue to follow the formula. After two hours, they are at the final stage of crystallization. Once crystallizing is complete, they are left with ten grams of a white, chalky substance.

"Shit, I hope that plant worked," he says.

"Yeah, me too, JJ. Me too."

"How much should we test?"

"Like, per dose?" George asks. "Well, I guess we start off at 10mg and make our way to 300mg."

"If it works, anyway," he adds.

George begins to laugh. "Where's your test subject at?"

"Shit, Mark is running around somewhere... I'll find him tonight. What are you doing tonight? You want to come over?"

"Yeah, that's cool. We'll find Mark and have him test this stuff...but yeah, we can just chill. I have to stop by my place and get some stuff first and drop off that money, but then I'll be over."

"Okay, that's cool." He scans the room and continues. "Let's get this place cleaned up so we can get out of here."

George bags up the white powder, and they clean up their make-shift lab, storing everything neatly away. They finish, and JJ grabs the bag and pockets it before leaving.

-----

JJ returns to his apartment and finds Mark and Amy chilling on the couch. "Hey guys," he says as he walks in.

"Hey JJ," Amy says. Mark nods.

"What are you guys doing tonight?" he asks.

"Nothing, probably. Why, what's up?" Mark asks.

"Well, I got some new stuff from someone and want to see if it works."

"JJ, the last time I tried the new stuff you had, it didn't do anything to me," Mark replies.

"Well, try this one," he urges, tossing the bag on the table. He turns and heads to his room to grab his digital scale. He returns and places the scale on the table. He takes out his ID card for a removable surface and pours the white powder, weighing out fifty milligrams. "This is good. Here Mark, try this." He hands the ID to Mark.

Mark takes the card and licks off the white powder. He grabs a nearby glass of water and drinks it down. "Oh God, that was nasty tasting...a lot worse than last time," Mark says, cringing.

Mark places the card back onto the scale, and JJ begins pouring out another fifty milligrams of powder. He hands it to Amy, and she licks it off the ID. Less than five seconds later, she is having the same reaction as Mark. "Oh God, this is nasty," she mumbles as she downs her own drink. She inhales after her long drink. "That is way worse than the taste ecstasy normally gives you... What is this supposed to do?" she asks.

"Well, I'm not sure exactly... My buddy told me it's supposed to be a good high, though," he replies.

"I guess we will see then," she says.

-----

Twenty minutes pass with no result. He looks at them. "Still nothing?" he asks. They shake their heads. JJ stands, curious at the situation. "Let me know if you start to feel it," he says before leaving the room.

"Okay," Mark replies.

He heads to his room and grabs his phone to call George. "Hey man, where you at?" he asks.

"I'm still at home. I'm almost ready to come over. Why? What's up?" George asks.

"I'll talk to you when you get here. How long are you thinking?"

George takes a brief pause to think. "Oh...probably half an hour to an hour, tops."

"Okay, I'll unlock the door. Just come in."

"Okay, I'll see you soon."

"Alright, I'll see you later," he replies, then hangs up.

Another twenty minutes pass, when he hears someone enter the apartment and begin talking to Mark and Amy. "George! I'm back here!" he yells from his room.

George steps into his room and closes the door. "Hey, so what's up that you needed to talk to me about?" George asks. "Did you give that stuff to Mark?"

"Yeah, that's what I wanted to tell you. I gave both Mark and Amy fifty milligrams each, almost an hour ago...and nothing has happened yet."

George sits down on the bed. "Maybe they didn't take enough... Maybe it's like how the ecstasy compound, low doses work. The more you take, the more the intensity and the effect on the body."

"Yeah, that could be the case," he responds.

"Let's just wait it out and see if anything happens," George says with reassurance.

They start looking up stuff on the Internet, going into research mode, when they hear Mark yell.

"JJ! Come here!"

Both of them get up and rush to the living room. "What's up, Mark? You feeling anything?" he asks.

"Yeah, a little bit…like that coming up feeling from ecstasy pills, but Amy is feeling it hard, though," Mark replies, looking at Amy.

JJ sits down in a chair while George heads towards the refrigerator. "So, when did it hit you?" he asks Amy.

"Just a few minutes ago," she replies.

"Try to explain the feelings…if you see anything…whatever it's doing to you," he says.

"It's hard to explain… I feel body rushes…euphoric feelings…but I see visuals and trails, too… I also can feel the dopey feeling…yet it's speedy and full of energy," she says slowly, trying to find the right words.

"Is it uncontrollable…the feelings, the sensations?" he asks.

"No, that's what's weird… If I concentrate, they all stop. But if I relax and let my mind wander, it just consumes me."

"Do you feel it affecting your motor functions at all?" he asks.

"What do you mean? Like my arms and legs and body

movements?"

"Yeah, exactly. Do you feel you've lost the control of your body parts so that they can't function normally?" he prods.

"Well, the sensations fill my body with the euphoric feelings, but it goes away when I do something, then takes over after I'm done doing what I was doing."

"Do the feelings and the high scare you, like a bad trip?"

"No, it's actually fun, because it feels like I have the power to control it and what happens."

"I want to be on her level," Mark says, frowning.

"Let's get you another fifty milligrams. It might be because you're bigger and you need more." He turns to Amy. "Would you be willing to take another fifty milligrams to see what it will do?"

"Yeah, I'll try it," she replies.

He repeats the process, weighing out another fifty milligrams for Mark then another fifty for Amy. "Okay, I'll let you guys go… Let me know if you feel anything, Mark."

"Okay, I will," Mark assures.

JJ turns to George. "Come on George, let's chill in my room."

They head back to his room, and he closes the door behind them. George sits down. "So you gave them one hundred milligrams total of that, right?" he asks.

JJ nods. "Yeah."

"I think its effects are based on weight," George replies. "Amy looked like she was way high off just fifty milligrams, but Mark seemed hardly effected... It might be like 2C-B or 2C-I though, and if you take too much, your body won't be able to handle it."

"Yeah, that's why I asked Amy to take the extra fifty milligrams to see, because it might have to be sold based on weight."

"That's going to be hard for us," George says with slight waver.

"I know; I hope it's not like that," he says.

-----

An hour passes this time, when they hear a female moan coming from the living room. They sneak up the hallway and look around the corner to find Amy riding Mark like a cowgirl.

"It must've worked for Mark," George whispers.

"Yeah, and for her too," he whispers back.

George smiles. "Yeah, you're right."

They sneak back down the hallway to JJ's room and close the door.

"Well, it looks like we did it!" George says in an excited voice.

"We either just created the new super drug or a new his-and-hers Viagra," he replies as they both start to laugh.

"So, what do you want to call it?" George asks.

"Well, from the looks of Mark and Amy, let's call it BLISS." He pauses. "But George, how would it be written scientifically?" he asks.

"Well JJ, using the compounds we did, if we were to write it out scientifically, it would probably look like this." George finds a piece of paper and begins writing. He finishes, then shows it to JJ. "This is how it would be written: 6-chestiamp-methyldiophit, and it would be pronounced chess-t-amp methill-die-off-fit," George says with a big grin.

"Wow, George," he says while shaking George's hand. He points to the poster of Alexander Shulgin. "We are now the parents to a new super drug," he says proudly.

George smiles and laughs. "Yes we are, JJ! You have just been Blissed." They both laugh again.

"But, George, first things first. Before we start selling it, we need to do more tests. We need to make sure it's safe."

George nods in agreement. As they sit in his room, celebrating their new creation, all he can seem to think about are the endless possibilities.

*This world is ours for the taking, and no one will be able to stop us now!*

# ABOUT THE AUTHOR

B. A. Talarico was born in Des Moines, IA. He had dreams of being a fighter pilot, but hit a speed

bump in his life and soon found a new friendship with co-author, Smurf. This is Talarico's first

novel and his introduction into the world of fiction novels.

*Smurf requested not to be mentioned in the Bio.

You can find more information about B.A. Talarico and the Bliss series at this sources:

Instagram: @blissthebook

Facebook: https://www.facebook.com/thebookbliss

Twitter: @blissthebook

Also please if you enjoyed my novel Bliss, please take a few minutes to go and write your review. Thank You!

www.ingramcontent.com/pod-product-compliance
Lightning Source LLC
Chambersburg PA
CBHW071211250626
47159CB00001B/277